Sexiful Rose

Sexiful Rose
Part 1

Clara Williams

Copyright © Clara Williams

All rights reserved. No part of this book may be reproduced in any form or by any electronic or mechanical means, including information storage and retrieval systems, without permission in writing from the publisher, except by reviewers, who may quote brief passages in a review.

ISBN: 978-1-64826-545-7   (Paperback Edition)
ISBN: 978-1-64826-546-4   (Hardcover Edition)
ISBN: 978-1-64826-544-0   (E-book Edition)

Some characters and events in this book are fictitious. Any similarity to real persons, living or dead, is coincidental and not intended by the author.

This is a work of fiction. Names, characters, places and incidents either are the product of the author's imagination or are used fictitiously, and any resemblance to any actual persons, living or dead, events, or locales is entirely coincidental.

Book Ordering Information

Phone Number: 347-901-4929 or 347-901-4920
Email: info@globalsummithouse.com
Global Summit House
www.globalsummithouse.com

Printed in the United States of America

This book is dedicated to my daughter, Tia; Sylvia and Jahi; Al and Shakiel; and Mom, I love you.

ACKNOWLEDGMENTS

I would like to give thanks to God first for giving me the willpower, strength, and patience to make this all a reality. I would like to thank my family for their unbridled support and helpfulness. I'd like to thank my team and everybody at Xlibris. Thank you all for making this book possible. Thank you.

I thank all of SitNet members especially my daughter, Tia, for being herself and being there when I needed a shoulder to cry on late at night when I was tired. She also made me believe in myself when no one else did. Thanks, Tia. My grandson, Shakiel, for keeping me grounded and staying on point and for keeping me on my toes and reminding me to move forward with my writing; Sylvia, my sister, for always giving me love, confidence, and support. Thank you for taking the time from your organization to lift me up when I was down and out.

My sister is the president, founder of Survival Instinct—The Network Inc.; and her husband, Jahi, is the vice president, cofounder of the organization. SitNet promotes cancer awareness, and I am so very proud to be a part of this wonderful organization. I would also like to take this time to thank my brother-in-law, Jahi, for believing in me.

Al, I want to thank you for being so patient and allowing me to work on this book without being interrupted. Al, sometimes you did fall under the category of people seeking little attention. I guess you could call that love!

I would like to thank a friend, who is an author, for guiding and directing me to write and to stay focused on this book.

Congratulations, Lil Bit, on your marriage and your beautiful twin boys. Thanks, Bit, for everything.

Thanks, Ali, for always being there when I didn't know where to turn. When something was wrong with my computer, you were there to guide me in whatever software that I needed to work with.

I would like to thank my cousin Zadie from Atlanta for being there for me when I would call her late at night for advice or just to talk about positive things.

I saved the best for last:

To my mother, I would like to take this time to thank you for your patience and understanding and being there when I needed your love and encouragement to go forward with my writing. Thanks, Mom.

I would like to take this time to thank God and all of you that will purchase my book. God bless!

Thank you, God!

PROLOGUE

La'Roc Rose (Sexi)

Sexiful is a high-profile lawyer. She is rated the best lawyer in the country.

Sexi falls in love with her soul mate, Shawn Parker. He makes her feel like a teenager again.

He gives her a feeling that she had never felt before. Sexiful never had a teenage life. Her family was too poor to buy Christmas toys or clothing for her and her siblings.

Sexi (short for Sexiful) makes a promise to herself that she or her family would never be hungry and they would always have everything they needed. She also makes another promise that her children would never want for anything for as long as she lives and after she is dead and gone.

Sexi's birth name: La'Roc Rose.

Shawn is fifteen years younger than La'Roc. Shawn always says, "Age is just a number, babe."

Shawn owns a real estate company. Sexi is the love of his life.

Sexi's daughter, Courtney, is in college studying to become a pediatrician; she is also a top model.

Courtney has a teenage son, Devon. Devon is a part-time model and a full-time student at Coward University. Devon and his mother have a good relationship as mother and son as well as friends.

Courtney is a slim and attractive young woman. She is tall, just like her mother. Courtney is very intellectual and wise in terms of understanding Sexi's love for Shawn. She always says, "Do what makes you happy, Mom."

Justin comes from a well-off family. Justin's father is allegedly responsible for his wife's death. Sexi believes that Justin's father is a low-down, dirty bastard, and he will pay for what he has done to his family.

Chantal and Denise are Sexi's best friends. They went to college together, and they were roommates all through college.

They ate from the same bowls, drink from the same glasses, and even sleep on the same bed. They have a bond that could never be broken. Growing up, they had nothing. All three of them came from poor families. Both are the godparents of Courtney and Devon.

Jordan has been a dear friend for years. He is always there for his friend La'Roc. They were also friends in college / law school. Jordan is the golden child. His family is rich. He was always blessed with money.

He was their savior in college. He is very dear to the three of them. (He has contacted HIV from a one-night stand.)

La'Roc's sister and her husband—they play a positive part in Courtney and Devon's life.

La'Roc's mother is a well-educated woman when it comes to her children and the people that become involved in her children's life.

Alex is a good friend as well as La'Roc's law partner.

Sexi trusts Alex with her life. If La'Roc ever needed a good lawyer, she would have the best there is, which means Alex. He is the second top-rated lawyer in the country.

Roger, Sexiful's ex-boyfriend, is a second-rate lawyer who never won a case.

April is Shawn's sister and Carlotta's best friend. Carlotta Brown is the mother of Shawn's son.

Oh, don't forget Paris and Biscuit, La'Roc's puppies. Ms. Cotton and Ms. Holiday are La'Roc's employees.

NEW YORK CITY

Saturday, March 31, 2008. Twelve noon. Dark clouds covered the sky, and the rain came down like a waterfall; but in Sexiful's heart, the sun was shining bright. It's as she almost felt it; today she would meet her soul mate.

Three weeks ago, falling in love was the last thing on her mind. But today, she felt love in the air—she felt it. Sexiful Rose felt beautiful today. She lounged in her Fifth Avenue apartment on her king size bed, wearing yellow sweatpants and a tight-fitting short-sleeved T-shirt. She had a half-eaten container of butter pecan ice cream in one hand and her TV remote control in the other. La'Roc was watching her favorite program on Lifetime when, suddenly, her seventy-two-inch plasma TV screen flickered, then went blank. She pointed the remote at the TV and mashed the Power button with her thumb over and over, but the screen remained blank. La'Roc checked the wires that connected the TV as if she knew what the problem was, but still no picture. It seemed she would have to write her own ending for that movie because the flat screen she had purchased some years back was not having it; it seemed it have had enough playtime.

While noticing the expression on Paris's face, La'Roc nearly dropped the almost-empty container of ice cream on her beautiful shag-carpet; she thought, *Paris, you better act like you know who feeds you.* So frustrated with her TV, she knocked the cordless handset off the nightstand beside her bed. "Damn, channel 45 is the only fucking channel that is worth watching on TV on a Saturday! How could this happen?"

Pissed off and feeling a bit clumsy for dropping the phone and nearly knocking out one of Paris's eyes with the remote, she reached down and grabbed the phone and muttered, "Maybe the only way I will meet the man of my dreams will be just that—*in my dreams!*" As she dialed the numbers to call Cablevision for repair, Paris just sat quietly and watched to be sure he was ready to move in the event she tossed anything else his way. After being on hold for approximately five minutes, a representative answered, "This is Cablevision. May I have the phone number for the service you are calling about?" After giving all the information requested and explaining the problem to the representative, La'Roc was told that a technician would be coming to her home the next day between 11:00 a.m. and 2:00 p.m. "Now what am I going to do in this house alone without a TV for the entire day?" she said out loud. "What can I do with all of this bottled-up anger?" She decided to take Paris out for a drive. "Come, Paris, let's go for a drive, boo."

She and Paris hopped into her cherry red Lexus SUV. Driving on the open road always brought about a sense of calmness to La'Roc. Along the drive, she spotted what seemed to be a quiet park and thought it would be a perfect spot to allow Paris to run and to prepare her opening remarks for an upcoming case the following Monday. The grounds were a bit wet from the earlier rain, but there was a covered bench that had La'Roc's name written all over it. As soon as she parked her Lexus and opened the door, Paris dashed out onto the damped grass. La'Roc gathered her law books and other needed materials that she'd hope would help build her case and walked to the park bench she had eyed as she was driving into the park. She placed Paris on a fifteen-inch leash, which gave him some freedom to roam while she hit the books. For nearly two hours, she focused only on her case while Paris slept. After preparing for her case, she and Paris ran around in the damped grass for another half hour. "Come on, Paris, let's go home." Remembering she had eaten the last bit of ice cream at home, she made one quick stop to the ice cream parlor.

The ride home was fast, and La'Roc was tired and in need of a nice hot shower. She parked her SUV and raced into the house. She noticed the light blinking on her answering machine and quickly hit the Play Message button as she turned on her shower. It was Cablevision calling to confirm the appointment for repair. Hearing the message reminded her of her nonworking TV, and feeling an oncoming sense of anger, she stripped and got into the shower. The hot water from her Kohler shower faucet was just what she needed to relieve some stress.

For the next fifteen minutes, there were no worries, no broken televisions, or anything wrong. After showering, La'Roc grabbed her laptop and a drink and headed into her bedroom to continue preparing for her big case on Monday

Being a defense attorney was one of her major accomplishments; she took real pride in her work, and she was damn good at it—even if she has to say so herself. After several hours of prepping, she decided to call it a night. She packed up her laptop and got in her comfortable king-size bed and shuffled herself under the soft, plush comforter, which she purchased from Lord & Taylor's two weeks ago, and drifted off to sleep.

La'Roc woke to the sound of her house phone blaring in her ears. Why, she wondered, did it feel as though she was waking up with the exact same hangover she had two months back at the Attorneys Charity Fundraiser Ball when she had way too many sips of champagne when all she did yesterday was prepare for trial, run in the park with Paris, and sip on one soothing drink? This certainly was not her ideal way to wake up. Still half asleep, which was evident in the way her voice sounded, she managed to get out a hello.

"Hi, this is Shawn Parker from cable to repair your TV. May I speak to Ms. Rose?"

"This is she," answered La'Roc.

Shawn continued, "I have a work order to repair your cable box. Would it be okay if I came over to your home in about fifteen minutes?"

La'Roc asked, "Today? Isn't it Sunday?"

Shawn responded, "Yes, Ms. Rose, its Sunday. I work as a private contractor and do a lot of business on Sundays. However, if today is not good for you, I can come on another day."

La'Roc cleared her throat and said, "It's just that I was expecting you on Monday, but no, no, today is good. I was thinking Monday. I will see you soon." Still a bit disorientated from the loud ringing of the phone, La'Roc still wondered why Cablevision would send a contractor out for repair on a Sunday *and* so damn early on a Sunday. Taking a quick glance at the clock hanging on her bedroom wall, she realized it was 11:45 AM, "He's not early, its noon." She shrugged her shoulders and said, "But still, it's Sunday."

She smiled to herself as she went into the bathroom to brush her teeth and wash her face. Searching through her closet for something to wear, she spotted a pair of her most comfortable Juicy Couture sweatpants. No sooner than she pulled the Couture's above her waist, John from building security was calling on the intercom. "Ms. Rose, there is a Shawn Parker from John's Cablevision to see you. Shall I send him up?"

"Yes, thank you," replied La'Roc. She quickly threw on a shirt and stood near the front door to await Mr. Sunday Morning Working Shawn. Was this a dream, La'Roc thought, or was this the finest man she'd ever laid eyes upon? With a welcoming smile, La'Roc invited him in.

"My name is Shawn Parker. I'm a cable technician from John's Cablevision," he said as he extended his hand to give her his business card. He stood approximately six feet, five inches tall and was built like nobody's business. Mr. Sunday Morning Working Shawn wore his hair in its natural state and did so much justice to the pair of jeans he wore. After greeting him, she led the way into her bedroom; she couldn't help but think to herself, *Wow, what a hunk of a man!* She showed him the television as he began to work, and she watched and watched and watched. From time to time, she would close her eyes for a moment and begin daydreaming about this man and how they would make love on her white cherry wood kitchen table.

"Ms. Rose," she heard her name called once, but she was so deep into her fantasy world that all she could do was moan, "Ahh." He called her name a second time, and this time it brought her back to reality. "Ms. Rose, is everything okay?"

"Oh, I'm sorry, I was just thinking about my book club." *What a horrible, pitiful lie*, she thought to herself and hoped he hadn't noticed how embarrassed she'd become. She was daydreaming about him—Mr. Sunday Morning Working Shawn, the repairman! "Did you find the problem?" she asked, trying to change the subject.

"Yes, I did," Shawn replied. "You just had a couple of wires tangled and unplugged here and there. I'm not going to charge you for that, and its time you updated your remote control, and until you do, your TV will continue to shut itself off every now and then."

"Oh, thank you, Mr. Parker. Now does this mean all three TVs are now in working order?"

"Yes," stated Shawn. She could feel his eyes piercing through her body as she walked away and headed to her living room to escort him out. He followed her and complimented her on how beautifully her coop was decorated.

"I decorated it with lots of love," said La'Roc.

"I see," said Shawn. He gave her a work order to sign, which she did, and returned it to him. "Thanks. Oh, by the way, Ms. Rose, I don't usually do this, but I can't help it . . . would it be okay that I hold on to your phone number to call you sometime, or is there another number where you can be reached?"

"Why? What are you going to become? My personal contractor?" asked La'Roc.

"I don't see why not," Shawn replied.

This is probably not a good idea, La'Roc thought. "Yes, you can call me at either number you have on file every now and then to make sure my cable is in working order, how's that?"

"Sounds like a plan," said Shawn.

La'Roc opened her front door as Shawn stood staring deep into her eyes. "It was a pleasure meeting you, Ms. Rose."

"It was a pleasure meeting you Mr. Parker."

"Please call me Shawn."

La'Roc took a deep breath as she locked her door and smiled with a gleam in her eyes.

After Shawn left, she walked into the bathroom and prepared herself for a long and hot bubble bath. Before diving in, she decided to pour herself a nice drink because after that encounter with that handsome young man, she needed a double shot of something—anything—but something quick. She decided to have a glass of Nuvo on the rocks. Trying to get Shawn out of her mind, she drifted back to a day several months ago when she took a trip to Paris with a good friend who, while there, introduced her to a drink called *Nuvo L'esprit de Paris Sparkling Liqueur.* Since her first taste, this had been her number one drink. She sipped and thought about getting in the whirlpool to chill out—or cool off might be more accurate. "You know what? Forget about the bubble bath, whirlpool it will be," she said aloud.

Sipping on her Nuvo, she stepped into her whirlpool. She felt relaxed though a bit exasperated with herself for having such thoughts about the cable guy. "Oh hell, I'll never see him again, but if I did . . . ooh boy," she said, talking to her most trusted companion, Paris, her Yorkshire terrier. Paris had been La'Roc's confidant since he was given to her as a birthday gift from a friend, and since that time, La'Roc had been holding meaningful conversations with him each and every day for nearly two years now. Paris was loved and spoiled as hell—I mean, to the core; and he loved it when La'Roc caressed his all-white fur, which, she noticed, went very well with the thick white carpet on her living room floor. Smiling, she looked around her coop and thought, *this place is beautiful and meticulously decorated—damn, I'm good!* Her town house in Westchester County and condo in the Bronx were also decorated just as beautiful. Attention had been paid to every detail. Each living quarters had a different personality, color, and style of its own—just the way La'Roc wanted. She thought those decoration classes during her spare time really did pay off.

After an hour, she stepped out of the whirlpool, feeling good and no thoughts of anything in particularly. No thoughts of Shawn, the cable technician repairman, or his body. She walked into her bedroom and moisturized her body all over with Keri Shea butter, which made her body feel smooth and soft. Her skin was like soft velvet. She had never used makeup a day in her life. Her skin was simply flawless.

La'Roc walked into her oversized master bedroom closet to find something to wear, and her search was over when she spotted a black V-neck blouse and a pair of tight black jeans. She completed her look with a pair of purple heels and a purple Louis Vuitton shoulder bag. Once dressed, La'Roc let her silky shoulder-length hair down and admired herself once more in the mirror before going out into the world, and said, "Yes, you go, girl. Mr. Sunday Working Cable Guy wished he could be so lucky." After dressing herself, she lifted Paris from his sofa and dressed him in his black jacket, then placed him into his Louis Vuitton purple-and-black doggie bag and headed to her SUV that was parked in her four-car garage.

She got into her Lexus and headed toward I-95 south with no special place in mind, just driving. The wind was a bit high, which made her hair blow and sway from side to side and back to back. La'Roc had other things on her mind, and the wind was not a part of what she was thinking.

She drove for hours and decided to stop at a diner called Carol's Place. She was in luck because dogs were allowed to go into the park.

While parking her SUV, she noticed another SUV parked two cars down from where she had parked. It was the same color, make, and model. "Oh well, Paris, let's take a walk in the park." As she started to walk, she heard someone call her name.

"Ms. Rose." She turned to see who called her and prayed it wasn't someone from her office because she simply did not want to talk shop today. "Ms. Rose!" the person yelled again.

La'Roc then recognized the person to be, guess who? Mr. Parker. "Hello, Mr. Parker."

"Please call me Shawn. It's a pleasure to see you again, Ms. Rose."

"Okay, Shawn, you can call me La'Roc." She felt herself beginning to blush as they made small talk about her TV and the weather.

"So everything is okay in TV land, right? No more issues?"

"No, everything is fine, Shawn, thank you." *His voice, his smile, his laughter . . . oh my god, I have to get away from this man*, La'Roc thought. Glancing at her Bulova wristwatch, she noticed the time and said, "Well, we really should get going."

"But you've just arrived, what's the rush?"

"I have an early call tomorrow." La'Roc and Paris left Shawn standing there, and she could feel his eyes burning into her soul as she walked away. She and Paris headed back to the SUV.

Driving home, all she could think of was Mr. Sunday Morning Working Shawn. He was the most charming man she'd ever met. "Okay, no time for him!" She forced her mind to be on the case she had to present in court in two days. She headed north on I-95. She felt a slight chill, so she closed the sunroof and pressed down on the gas. She was passing everything on the highway. She looked over at Paris, who was falling asleep. "You had a hard day too, huh? Okay, buddy, we will be home shortly." She put in a CD, "Send for Me" by Atlantic Starr; she liked track 2. The music was so loud it woke Paris up from his sleep. She later popped in Anthony Hamilton's "Can You Feel Me?" She was in a hurry to get started on her presentation.

Tired from driving and anxious to get out of her clothes, she decided to stay in Westchester and drive into the city the next day. By the time she pulled into her town house garage, it was about 9:30 p.m. She complimented herself on the short time it took her to get home and said to Paris, "Guess I was speeding a little bit, huh, babe?"

She g rabbed her companion and dashed for the front door. After undressing Paris and giving him his food, she walked into the sitting room to check her phone messages. The sitting room was beautifully colored and decorated in mauves and plums. She checked her messages. The first message was from her daughter.

"Hi, Mother, It's me, Courtney. I'm just calling to check up on you and wanted to see how things were going. Your grandson should be home from college soon. Call me back. I love you."

After taking some time off to raise her son, Courtney returned to college to pursue her medical degree. Now that she had graduated from med school, she and Courtney had much more time to spend with each other. The sound of her daughter's voice made her smile. She was so proud of her and the way that she'd turned out. She thought back to when she had offered to pay her daughter's school tuition and she refused—Ms. Independent. To make ends meet, Courtney began a modeling career and was highly requested by the agency's owner, Sarah, to model fashions made by top designers. She had been modeling for Sarah's modeling agency part-time for nearly three years. La'Roc's grandson also joined in the modeling industry. He was a part-time model with Raisins Modeling agency called I'm Running the Runway.

The second message was from Denise, her best friend. "Hi, sexy girl, where the hell are you? Call me, I need to talk to your black ass about this guy I met yesterday."

The last message was from her sister, L'Oreal. "Hey there, it's your sister, give me a call, I love you." Her sister was happily married to a wonderful man, Casey. They owned their own production company and were the presidents and founders of two businesses: one was ballroom dancing and the other was an event-planning business. They planned weddings, parties, and grand openings for the elite.

La'Roc picked up the phone and called her daughter first. There was no answer, so she left a short message. She then decided to call her mother.

"Hi, Mom."

La'Roc and her mother talked for at least an hour about everything under the sun. Noticing how late it was getting, she thought it was best to cut their conversation short. "Mom, I am going to have to bid you good night. I have a big court case in a few days that I need to prepare for, but I will give you a call tomorrow, okay."

"Okay, baby, you have a good night." And they both hung up. "Oh shit! I forgot I have a doctor's dermatologist appointment tomorrow." She mixed herself a drink and checked on Paris. He was fast asleep. She went upstairs and took a long hot shower. After she showered, she moisturized and pulled out a pair of Victoria's Secret boxers and a matching T-shirt.

She sipped on a drink and decided to take out an outfit for her appointment. She took out a pair of chocolate Guess jeans and a beige tank top. Going through her shoes, she decided on her three-inch beige Steve Madden heels. Thinking out loud, "Baby, I look good in whatever I wear," she pulled out a jacket to match her outfit. Pulling her hair back, she slipped under her comforter and drifted peacefully to sleep.

The next day, Paris woke her up as he did every morning.

"Paris, please, what time is it?"

Paris looked as if to say, "Hell! I have to go to the bathroom," as he used his cold nose to nudge her. She threw herself out of bed and put on her sweats and matching sweater and took Paris for his morning walk so he could relieve himself. When she returned, she popped in a CD and did her morning exercise and got dressed. After giving herself a once-over, she grabbed a glass of orange juice and a rice cake and headed out the door.

On her drive to the dermatologist, La'Roc thought back to her prior dermatologist whose schedule was always so backed up she would wait at least two hours before being seen. She had been blessed to have been referred to her new dermatologist because this particular doctor only scheduled five patients per day, which, of course, means shorter or no-wait periods. La'Roc made it on time for her appointment and waited for approximately fifteen minutes before being seen. She met with the dermatologist for about fifteen minutes and was told what La'Roc already knew—"Your skin is flawless." La'Roc left the doctor's office and went straight home to relax and enjoy her day off. Driving and mentally planning the rest of her evening, she was interrupted when her cell phone started to ring.

She checked the phone for a name to appear; the name never showed up on her phone. She decided to answer.

"Hello," she said into her Bluetooth headset.

"Hello, this is Shawn, your cable technician. How are you doing?"

"I am doing just fine, thank you."

"Are you at work?"

"No," she answered, puzzled as to why he was so curious about her work schedule.

"I was just wondering if I could stop by."

La'Roc wanted to yell to the mountaintop, "Hell yes!" but continued to act reserved and said, "My cable is working just fine, Shawn."

"But what about you, La'Roc, are you working just fine or do you need a tune-up?"

La'Roc let out a big laugh as Shawn continued to plead. Finally, she could not resist any longer. Not that she wanted to anyway, but she had to play the role of hard to get. "Yes, just for a minute."

Twenty minutes after she got in her door, Shawn showed up with a container.

"What's that?" she asked him.

"Well, I thought the reason you were home was because you were sick. So I bought you some vegetable soup," he explained.

Trying to hide her smile, she thought he was very thoughtful. They spent most of that day together—twenty minutes, yeah, right. He made it very clear that he wanted to get to know her better as a person, not as a Cablevision customer.

She admitted to herself that she wanted the same, but she remained cool. She pretended that she was not interested. He talked about his life, and she discussed her life and family. All her life she wanted to be special, and Shawn was doing just that; he made her feel special. He gave her more confidence, and most of all, he made her believe in herself. Throughout their conversation that day, La'Roc felt comfortable enough with Shawn to share one of her innermost secrets—she told him that her confidence was zero, no matter how confident she came across. It was all a cover-up.

Before Shawn, she was dating a trial lawyer, but they were on the verge of breaking up. They were together for many years. It was time for a change; the arguments were getting worse. He did not like the fact that she was making more money than he made, getting more important cases than he was getting. Shawn opened her eyes that evening, forced her to see herself as an individual and not as a "we." He looked into her eyes and told her, "You have a lot to offer. You need to believe in yourself. You are beautiful, sexy, smart, and very talented. You need to focus on yourself. You do not need a man to validate who you are."

"You don't understand. This guy took my self-esteem and almost broke me down to his level of thinking with his verbal and mental abuse."

Shawn was a very outspoken man. He looked at La'Roc and almost melted her heart with his sexy big brown eyes as he said, "I am a cable technician and proud of it. I am looking to start my own business one day, and that one day will be soon. I want to go into real estate. I know that you are a big-time lawyer and all that, and you're probably thinking that I am talking out of my head. La'Roc, I can take you to a place that you have never been. Just give me a chance to show you. I am not just a cable repairman. I have other things besides cable. I also own a realty company. I buy and sell houses to companies. I know you heard of Donald Mason. He is one the richest men in the world. He is one of my biggest buyers as well as Rodney Taylor. This guy, Rodney, he owns half of New York. So you see, I am not doing too bad, hon. I did not tell you about my realty company before because I wanted to see the expression on your face. Now that you know, I'm not that poor little cable guy. I am very attracted to you both physically and sexually."

He was talking, and she was fantasizing about the two of them making wild love in her office on her big Oakwood desk. He throws her to the floor from her desk in a rage of passionate intimacy. Her body hits the floor on the rust colored carpet as he makes rough love to her entire body. "La'Roc G. Rose, snap out of it!" she said to herself as she forced reality to settle in.

"I think you should leave now," she told Shawn.

"Yeah, it is about time." He got up to leave. "Oh, before I leave, I have a name especially for you. I'm going to call you Sexiful. You like that? That name is only for you, okay. Sexiful, don't you ever forget you are sexy and beautiful."

She blushed and closed the door behind him.

Her thoughts still on Shawn, she walked over to her bar and mixed herself a drink to relax before taking a hot bath. She undressed and settled down into her favorite chair. Her mind drifted back to earlier that evening when Shawn was making love to her body with his eyes and she wanted him to do more. Shawn was all she could think about during her bubble bath. She fell off to sleep in the bathtub. The whole time she was soaking, she was dreaming about Shawn to the conversation they shared earlier about not needing a man to validate who she was. The phone rang, disturbing her dream. She reached over and answered. A little annoyed, she said, "Hello. Who is this?"

"Hey, this is Shawn, just called to say good night."

"Good night, Shawn."

"Good night, Sexiful."

She jumped out of the bathtub like a teenager with a big smile on her face. She was a happy camper. A young man was calling her; how cute was that? She was fifteen years older than Shawn. When she told Shawn her age, he said, "I see you as a person, not how old you are. I want to spend time with you. Whatever happens." Butterflies flew around in her stomach.

"Okay, okay, focus. Time for a little work. Tomorrow is a long workday." She went into her study and sat down in front of her laptop to type her opening statement for her case. If she wins this case, she would be a million dollars richer. "Oh hell, what am I saying? I will win this case." Her confidence boosted a bit. She never lost a case before; why would she lose this one?

After briefly reviewing her notes, she mixed another drink and went into her closet to take out an outfit for her win the following day. She smiled to herself.

Searching through her closet, she decided to wear an off-white suit with dark green accessories, her three-inch green Marc Jacobs heels, matching green bag, and a big diamond ring on her middle finger. She placed the laptop on the marble end table in the foyer. "I am so ready for this case."

She put on a pair of sexy pajamas and jumped into bed.

It seemed as if she had just begun to dream when her phone rang. She opened her eyes, momentarily blinded by the bright morning sun shining through her blinds.

"Good morning, Sexiful. Are you all right?"

"Yes, is there something wrong?" she asked as she sat up on her bed.

"I just wanted to hear your voice."

"Thanks, good morning. Shawn, I have to get dressed for work. I will talk to you soon, okay? Bye." She jumped out of bed and headed for the bathroom; Paris started to bark and ran to the door. "Paris, Mommy isn't taking you for your morning walk. Ms. Holiday will be here in a few minutes. Please be patient, okay, babe?"

La'Roc ran into the bathroom, brushed her teeth, took a shower, and went into the bedroom to get dressed for work.

"Hi, Ms. Holiday, I thought I heard you come in. How're you this morning?" she said to her housekeeper.

"I am fine, thank you."

Ms. Holiday had been working for La'Roc for several years. She also traveled to Manhattan to clean the condo on the weekend. La'Roc loved the way Ms. Holiday worked—straight to business, always punctual, and she could also be trusted. There was a different housekeeper to clean the coop in the Bronx. La'Roc called her Ms. Cotton because her hair was white as white can be.

She pulled her hair back into a high ponytail. The ponytail, with her dark glasses on, made her look so damn sophisticated, she thought to herself. Saying her good-byes to Paris and Ms. Holiday, she headed to the garage. Looking at her cars, she decided to drive her BMW. She put on her sunglasses, got into her money green BMW, and drove away, as always, faster than a speeding bullet. That was La'Roc for you. She was always in a hurry when it came time to making money. Pulling into the parking garage, she grabbed her briefcase, pressed the alarm on her car, and headed to the courtroom. She walked into the courtroom with more confidence than any other lawyer in the room.

She loved the proceedings, every aspect of it. She introduced her client, Mr. Robertson, to the court. Mr. Robertson was being sued for a hit-and-run car accident. He was a tall Caucasian dressed in a dark gray suit, yellow shirt, and a gray tie with yellow background. His hair was salt-and-pepper colored. Giving him a once-over, she could tell that his suit was tailor-made just by looking at the pattern. He was well established in his profession; he was CPA on Wall Street. (La'Roc never met Mr. Robertson; she was called in on this case by the judge.)

After the opening statements, the judge adjourned the case until the next two days. "All parties are to return to court on Thursday," the judge exclaimed before heading off into the chambers.

Her mind wanderback to Shawn and the last two days they were together. Her ringing cell phone disturbed her thoughts. It was Shawn. She smiled as she answered the phone. He wanted to see her again. She couldn't contain her smile. It stretched from ear to ear. They made plans to meet up at her town house in Westchester County at five thirty that evening.

Wanting to share her new found joy with someone, she decided to call her friend Chantal. After several rings, she was forwarded to the voice mail. She left a message: "Paging Dr. Chantal! Hey, girl, give me a call when you get this message. I'm on a roll, if you know what I mean."

"Ugh. Let me call my girl Denise. Someone's got to hear this!" She dialed Denise's number. She picked up after the second ring. "Hello, girlfriend."

"Well, hello, Ms. Bitch, where the hell have you been?"

Denise sounded surprised. "I've been around, trying to get me a new man and get laid. I want to find me a young man like your men." La'Roc laughed. "Oh, I hear about you and your younger man. I was wondering when I was going to meet this hunk," Denise snapped back.

"Well, my friend, I would introduce you if he was my hunk. I am sorry to say he is not. He is just a friend, nothing more. I know that bitch Chantal told you about Shawn. That slut cannot, and I mean cannot, hold water!" La'Roc laughed out loud. "I will call you later. I have a date tonight."

"You have a date?" Denise asked eagerly.

"Yes, I do. Talk to you soon, bitch, got to go." She disconnected the call before Denise could finish her questions. She stepped on the gas and headed to her town house. Doing eighty miles per hour in her BMW on the highway, her hair blowing in the wind was just how she liked it. Her sunglasses on, she looked in the mirror and said to herself, "I'm the best lawyer in the world, and my interior decorating skills are off the hook." She flashed a smile and continued.

When she pulled up to her town house, it was just a little after three o'clock. A few more minutes until she would be in Shawn's arms where she will be the rest of her life if everything works out tonight like she planned. Tonight was her first official date with her dreamboat or, should she say, her boy toy. Her stakes are high; all bets were on her relationship tonight with Shawn.

Tonight, she would make love to Shawn like there had been no other man in her life until tonight.

She jumped out of her BMW and ran into the house, very excited about her date. Her first date with a man fifteen years her junior; she was terrified of what could happen in her bedroom that night, yet she was so excited. She undressed, put on a pair of sweats and a T-shirt, and started her exercise. Ms. Holiday had already taken Paris out for the evening. She had left a note to say that she and Paris would be going to the park. She finished her exercise and mixed a cold drink for herself.

Paris ran into the house at full speed. Ms. Holiday ran right behind him and headed into the gym where she was lying on her mat, relaxing from doing her exercise. Paris jumped up, happy and excited to see his mother. She was extremely happy to see her baby as if they had been apart for years. That is what you called devotion.

"Ms. Holiday, are you available to work tonight?"

"Yes, I'm all yours. I like taking care of you and little Paris."

"I would like it if you could make dinner for me and a friend of mine." La'Roc ignored the smirk that began to spread across her housekeeper's face and walked into the bathroom.

"Ms. Rose, what are we having for dinner tonight?"

La'Roc, yelling from the bathroom, replied, "Fish salad, and put a bottle of champagne on ice, no desert. Ms. Holiday, please set up dinner in the small dining room. Don't forget the candle and appropriate lighting. It's sort of a special night. Also, could you please give Paris his bath and his snack? Thanks."

After soaking in her whirlpool for a bit, she glanced at the time. "Wow! It's five fifteen. I need to start getting dressed!" She went to her walk-in closet, pulled down her sexy black gown with a low-cut V-neck down to her naval and a built-in bra and black sling-back heels. She topped it off with her hair in a sexy, messy bun right on the top of her head.

Her body looked so damn toned and she looked so fucking sexy in whatever she wore. "Shawn will fall in love with me tonight, or he is gay," she said, smiling to herself.

At five forty-five, the front gate intercom rang. "Ms. Holiday, will you please answer the intercom?"

"Who is it?" Ms. Holiday spoke into intercom.

"Shawn Parker."

"Ms. La'Roc, it's a Mr. Parker." She smiled.

"Please open the gate for him."

Moments later, the doorbell rang. She heard Shawn say, "Hello, my name is Shawn Parker."

"Please, Mr. Parker, come in and have a seat. Ms. Rose will be with you shortly. Would you like a drink?"

"No, thank you."

After putting the final touches on her hair, she walked into the room where Shawn was waiting. Shawn, who was sitting on the couch, rose to his feet when she entered the room, and he looked at her like she was the only woman in the world. She knew then that she had accomplished what she set out to do.

The gaze in his eyes gave the impression of being in love. The expression on his face said, "I want only you to be in my life forever."

"Hello, Shawn, glad you could make it," she said, putting on the sexiest voice she could muster.

"Sexiful, you look fantastic. How do you keep yourself in shape?"

"I work out a lot and eat appropriately."

"You got it going on, babe."

She smiled and walked over to the table where Ms. Holiday had everything set out so beautifully. After dinner, they had drinks by the glow of the fireplace.

Shawn held her in his arms while they listened to a slow CD. Soft music from Atlantic Starr, Robert Thicke, the Magic Touch, and the sound of the music filled the room.

"Sexiful, do you believe in yourself, and do you believe that together, we could make this happen? Please give me a chance to show you and let me take you to a place that you have never experienced before. I have a spaceship that is waiting to take you away into my paradise. I will treat you like the queen that you are. Sexiful, let me love you."

"No, Shawn. Please give me some time." Her heart said yes, and her body was on fire. She needed him as much as he needed her. But she could not allow herself to make love to Shawn at that moment. Shawn pulled her into his arms and held her so tightly that she could not breathe. "Oh, baby, stop, you are hurting me. I want you more than ever, but this is not the right time. I am afraid of getting hurt. Shawn, please try and understand, and there is a big difference in our age."

"I promise you I will never hurt you, and I really don't think about our age. I know you're always thinking about the age thing. That is the farthest thing from my mind. What say you? Let's give it a shot, okay, sweetheart. Take a chance. You are a trial lawyer, you gamble every day. Let's gamble on our love," he said. "I am going to leave and give you some time to think about us. I won't rush you into anything. I will wait forever if I have to."

"Shawn, please don't leave, stay with me tonight," she said, giving in.

"Baby, are you sure?"

"Yes, I am sure," she admitted.

Shawn smiled. "I will just hold you in my arms all night, and I will love you from afar. Sexiful, I want you, and I am willing to wait as long as it takes. I will wait until you are ready. I could fall in love with you tonight. I think I already have."

She stood and beckoned for Shawn to follow her. She began to walk toward her Jacuzzi. He followed closely behind with his arms around her small waist. Once they entered the Jacuzzi room, she turned and looked him in the eyes and said, "Shawn, I am glad that you're here tonight."

She dropped her black gown to the floor as he dropped his clothing next to hers. He took her hand and led her into the Jacuzzi. He stepped in, and she followed and sat in front of him with his strong arms around her waist.

He began to caress her body all over. He kissed her like she had never been kissed before.

She loved his strong arms around her. He took her to a place that she had never gone before. She had never been loved like he loved her that night. He made love from her head to her toes. "Baby, I will be gentle. Just relax and let daddy make love to you."

She fell deeply into his spell. It was all good because she was in Shawn's heaven and loving every moment of it.

His lovemaking was so amazing she cried all through their passionate night because she never had anyone to make love to her like Shawn was making love to her that night.

She knew that night was the beginning of a beautiful and a wonderful relationship.

Stepping out of the Jacuzzi, he held her close to his wet body, and she felt like a limp wet rag. She couldn't speak.

Shawn holding her made her speechless. After making love in the Jacuzzi with Shawn, she was helpless. He picked her up and carried her to her master bedroom and asked her if she wanted a drink.

"Yes, please."

He came back into the bedroom with two drinks in his big hands and a towel wrapped around his body.

Wow! She wanted more and more of that good-looking, gorgeous man that was entering her bedroom. He looked so damn good she wanted to keep him in her life forever.

He sat down on the side of the bed. "Hi, beautiful, you okay?" he asked sincerely.

"Yes, baby, I am fine."

He handed her a drink, and they toasted each other. After they finished their drinks, they were both ready for bed. He asked her to sleep on his chest all night. She obliged and slept on his chest with no regrets.

The next morning, Paris ran into the master bedroom and jumped into the bed. Shawn kept his cool. Although Paris frightened the hell out of him, he didn't show it. They both looked at each other and laughed. La'Roc called Ms. Holiday to retrieve Paris from her room.

"I am sorry, Ms. Rose." Ms. Holiday knocked on the door and then entered the bedroom. "Good morning. I am really sorry, Ms. Rose," she repeated as she picked up Paris.

"Good morning, Ms. Holiday," La'Roc replied, smiling.

"Good morning, Ms. Holiday," Shawn said.

Ms. Holiday left the room smiling. "Ms. Rose, would you like for me to make you and your guest breakfast?"

"Yes, please. Shawn, what would you like for breakfast?"

"I will have whatever you are having."

"I am having the usual—toast, coffee, and juice. That's okay, baby?"

Shawn nodded in agreement.

She and Shawn stepped into the shower, and he gazed into her eyes and said, "I want you. I want you to be with me for as long as you want me because right now, I want to be with you forever. Please tell me that you want me as much as I want you." She couldn't resist. She reached her hands up to his face, and his lips met hers aggressively; he kissed her long and passionately.

After breakfast, Shawn left for work. Before he left, he looked at her and said, "Come here." He kissed her on her lips. "Baby, it was great being in your arms last night. I would like to take you out to dinner tonight if you're available."

She smiled and said, "I'll call you later after I check my schedule."

Shawn was halfway out of the door when he said, "Okay, I will wait for your call. Keep it sweet."

She watched Shawn drive away. Her insides began to yearn for more of Shawn's heavy breathing as she reminisced about the way he made love to her the night before.

As she looked out of her window, she almost panicked because she thought that she saw her ex-boyfriend's jeep.

She called to Ms. Holiday and asked her to go down to the gate to find out if she was right. Ms. Holiday ran back into the house. "Yes, it is Mr. Harrison."

"Thank you, Ms. Holiday."

She could hear her cell phone ringing in the other room. She ran to answer it. "Hi, Shawn, miss me?"

"This is not your precious Shawn. This is Roger, we need to talk. There are some things we need to discuss."

La'Roc rolled her eyes as Roger spoke. "Roger, we said it all. I have nothing to say to you."

"Baby, please hear me out. I know I fucked up, but it has always been you and only you. You got to believe me."

"Roger, I don't have to do shit. What you need to do is to go on with your life because that is what I'm doing. Now you listen very carefully." She slammed the phone down as hard as she could.

Before she could lift her hand off the receiver completely, the phone rang again. She snatched up the phone. "Get tHe fuck off of my pHone!"

"Hi, babe, this is Shawn. What's wrong? Did I do something?"

"I am sorry, sweetheart. I just had an unfortunate encounter with my ex-boyfriend. I'll be all right, thanks for showing concern."

"You need me to come back to Westchester?" Shawn asked with a serious tone.

"No. I told you I am okay. How's your morning so far?"

"I am good. Have you thought about tonight?"

"No, I really haven't had a chance to check my schedule. Oh hell. Just give me a minute if you are not busy. I'll check now."

"Baby, I can wait as long as you need me to wait."

After checking her appointment book and making sure she didn't have to meet with any clients, she said, "Guess what? I am all yours tonight."

"Good. I will see you around six thirty or seven."

"Okay, babe." She disconnected the call. She could hear the faint buzz of the gate intercom from her bedroom. Ms. Holiday knocked on her bedroom door, then opened it.

"It's Mr. Harrison. Should I open the gate?"

"This damn man is getting on my fucking nerves. I need to speak to him to get him off my back," La'Roc mumbled to herself. "Ms. Holiday, yes, please give security permission to open the gate."

While waiting for Roger to get to the town house, La'Roc paced back and forth. She was trying to figure out what it was that he wanted. They had been apart for almost a year now.

Roger suddenly walked in. "Hi, sexy lady. How you been?"

"What is that you want from me, Roger?" she asked, rolling her eyes and placing her hands on her hips.

"What is your problem, La'Roc? I just wanted to stop by to say hello. Is that asking too much? We were together for several years, and I am just supposed to forget about what we had together?"

"Yes! I did, and I am going on with my life."

"Oh, I see, with your boy toy?" Roger said sarcastically.

"Is that a question, or are you just being an asshole? If you want to know something, please be a man and ask me. Yes, I have a man, and he is younger than I am, so what?"

"I feel like fucking you up!"

La'Roc huffed. "You know what I feel like doing? I feel like kicking your ass out of my house! You know what? Get out of my house before I put a bullet in your nasty ass, and you know that I will. So don't fuck with me, Roger. Please leave my town house!"

"This shit is not over. You will hear from me again," he mumbled in her ear as he walked past her.

"What the fuck are you mumbling in my ear? Whatever you just said, you better keep it to yourself and watch your back. Roger, that is not a threat. It is a promise. Now please, please leave me alone."

Wow! What a morning, she thought to herself. She walked to her bar to pour herself something strong. She finally decided on Grey Goose vodka with tonic water and some crushed ice. What she really needed to do was to call her baby. Shawn made her feel like a million dollars. She dialed his cell phone number.

"Hi, handsome, are you busy?" she asked when he picked up. "Sexiful, I am never too busy to speak to you."

"I just wanted to hear your voice," she said as she lounged back in her chair. And she truly meant it. Right now, all she needed was him.

"Hey, babe, what's wrong?"

"Nothing, I'm good," she lied. "Are we still on for tonight? I can't wait to be in your arms again and you loving me all over my body," she asked.

"Yes, Sexiful, of course. I will see you at 7:00 p.m. See you soon."

"Okay, we need to talk about an unexpected visitor that I had an encounter with this morning. See you at seven o' clock, okay, babe."

"See you at seven, Sexiful."

She hung up from Shawn and mixed herself a drink of tonic water, crushed ice, and vodka. Vodka had always relaxed her especially when she was around a no-winning lawyer like that damn fool, Roger. She had known Roger for several years, and since she had known him, he won only one case in court.

"I don't know how he became a trial lawyer. The man is dumb as hell and always trying to talk law in public," she thought aloud. She made more money than he did, and with her getting more clients than him, he saw that as being a threat to him and his ego. The fact that she was making more than him played a big part in their relationship not being stable. He would constantly try and put her down in front of their friends and their families.

Her friends, Chantal and Denise, and her sister, L'Oreal, could see straight through Roger; but she was so blinded by love she couldn't see his madness. Her friends have spoken to her on many occasions about Roger's jealousy.

Before she kicked Roger out of her coop, she noticed that everything she said or did, he would become defensive and resentful toward her. Chantal said one day, "Girlfriend, leave that motherfucker alone. If not, he will bring you down with him. Roger is going down, and he is trying to take you with him. He is a wannabe attorney. And since he can't be a better lawyer than you, he will destroy you one way or another."

She lounged in her chair and stared at the ceiling, trying to rid her thoughts of anything related to Roger. Looking at the clock, she noticed it was 2:30 p.m. *I have to get going*, she thought. Ms. Holiday had Paris at the vet all afternoon. She missed her boo today. As she stood up, she could hear her front door opening. At that moment, Ms. Holiday yelled from the kitchen, "We're back! Paris is on his way upstairs." Paris ran into her master bedroom and jumped up on La'Roc's back and almost pushed her to the floor, but she fell on the bed instead. She played with Paris for about thirty minutes. Afterward, he was so tired he went for his nap. She asked Ms. Holiday to pack her clothes because she needed her in Manhattan with her and

Paris. Ms. Cotton, her usual housekeeper for the Manhattan coop, was taking care of her mother this week. She was diagnosed with cancer several months ago, and she needed some time off. La'Roc continued to pay Ms. Cotton as long as she was out taking care of her mother. She gave her twelve months off with pay.

She took a shower. After she dried and moisturized, she ran to her walk-in closet to pick out an outfit to wear to Harlem that evening. She turned on her seventy-two-inch plasma TV that was mounted on her bedroom wall. She punched in channel 45 to watch a movie while she picked out her outfit. *Oh, I think Shawn will like this low-cut rust blouse with my signature denim jeans and three-inch denim heels.* She laid out her clothing for that night. Shawn liked the way she dressed, especially when she wore jeans. She remembered the time he pulled her into his chest and said, "Sexiful, you're the most beautiful woman I have ever dated. La'Roc, you have it all, and, babe, I respect you for all that you have accomplished. I like the way you dress, and, baby, you can dress your ass off."

She thanked Shawn and thought to herself *"yes I've worked very hard to accomplish what I have". I thank God every day for what I have obtained.*

Snapping back to reality, she grabbed her bag and ran out the door with her sweats on and a hoodie. Paris ran behind her. She opened the door, and Paris jumped in the Lexus. "Ms. Holiday, I'm going to get a manicure, facial, and a pedicure. I will be back in a few hours. Hell, I got to look good for Shawn. After all, this is our second real date." She giggled.

Usually, her manicure and pedicure were done at her home; however, today, she chose to go out to a salon to get her beauty treatments. She was interested in meeting other people other than lawyers, doctors, or realtors, which seemed to be the only professions in her circle. She couldn't remember the last time she had been to a salon. It was a beautiful day, and she drove at normal speed.

She smiled to herself as she looked over at Paris. "Love you, babe." Paris licked her face, then jumped in the backseat and stuck his head out of the window.

Her cell phone began to ring. She glanced at the screen; it was Shawn.

"Hi, Sexiful, where are you?"

"Hi, Shawn, I'm dropping Paris to the dog groomer, then I'll be on my way to the beauty parlor."

"Wow! You are going to a beauty salon?" He was laughing.

"What's so funny?"

"You are. We still on for tonight, right?" he asked.

"Of course we are, honey."

"Okay, see you then."

Their call ended just as she arrived at the salon. She was on time for her appointment. Although her hair was up in a ponytail, she pulled it down so it would flow in the wind. She loved it when her hair was free to blow out of control.

She walked into the salon, and all eyes were on her as she strutted her stuff across the floor. She knew every one of those bitches wished that they were her. But it was all good. She overheard one woman say, "Damn, that bitch's body is so fucking toned. I wonder what the hell she does every day!"

She turned around and looked at the woman. "Let me introduce myself. I am La'Roc Rose, and the answer to your question is this body comes from hard working out and being committed."

One lady said, "You look damn great, girl, and aren't nothing funny about me."

She thanked them for their compliments and walked over to Wanda, her stylist.

After getting her manicure, pedicure, and facial done, she decided to top off her day out with doing her hair. She asked her stylist to wash her hair and blow it out. After she was done, she paid and left her stylist a generous tip. She felt good walking out of the salon with other people that were not in her so-called circle. She felt like a regular person.

Driving back to her town house, she drifted back to when she was struggling back in high school. She was more than regular; she was poor. She believed in God, and she knew then that she was going to make it one day. She was accepted to Yule. She cried and prayed for the next few days because she heard God say, "La'Roc, you are going to be a great attorney." She knew that he spoke to her because she was not just the greatest but she was one of the best lawyers in the state of New York.

She thought about the times when her family lived in the South and they had nothing to eat. They were hungry most of the time. Her parents would try and make them forget food by playing family games such as hide-and-seek, bingo, old maid 500, and jump rope. Her father worked very hard to give them what they needed, not what they wanted. She always daydreamed that she was going to be a lawyer. Her father always called her his lawyer because she loved to talk. Her father looked at her and said, "One day, you will make a damn good mouthpiece." She often laughed about being a mouthpiece. It was difficult for her when she went to high school and college. During school, work was very difficult especially when they didn't have any electricity in the house. That was when she came to the conclusion that she would never be poor again and neither would her family. Her family couldn't afford to send her to college, so she would go with her friends and sit outside of the classroom and listen to the instructor teach. That was how she started her career. One day, while sitting in the hallway, the instructor Mr. Black asked her to join the class; she accepted his offer, and that was her first time going into a classroom of law. She would never forget Mr. Black. They still speak occasionally at least once or twice a month. She worked her way to the top of her profession as a lawyer. That is why today she looked back over her past and thank God for what she had accomplished.

Her first case was a little tough. That was the day she met Roger. Roger taught her a lot about law; however, he never won a case. She always found that so peculiar. He seemed so bright and informed of the law, yet he couldn't win a case to save his life. Her first big case was the talk of the country—a million-dollar case. There were no mistakes to be made. She had to win that one, and she did. She was defending the biggest judge in the country, embezzlement and tax fraud and a whole lot more. Of course, he walked; the prosecution just didn't have enough evidence to convict. After that, she was called one of the best lawyers in the state of New York. Two years later, she opened up her own firm, La'Roc Law Firm.

She made her parents and sibling millionaires. She smiled to herself as she remembered how far she'd come.

Looking at the time on her car radio, she figured Paris would be finished with his appointment and was ready for pickup. She pulled up in front of the store. The door chimed as she opened it. The owner, recognizing her, went to the back and came back with Paris in his hands.

"Come, Paris, we got to move. It's getting late." She thanked and paid the groomer, then headed toward her SUV. She put Paris in the backseat, put on her glasses, and continued on the last leg of her journey home to prep for her date.

Excited and eager to get home, she blazed down the highway, clocking eighty miles an hour. "Almost home, baby, because we have a big date tonight, right?" she said to Paris. He licked his lips and turned away. Paris was always a little angry after just getting a haircut. "I am sorry, baby. Mommy still loves you." She laughed to herself and continued to speed toward I-95 North to get to the expressway to her town house in Westchester County. She put in a CD by Alicia Keys.

She slowed at a yield sign and noticed a van was behind her, trying to get her attention. When she was able, she pulled off. The van continued to follow her. She stopped at the first gas station exit to check out the motherfucker that was following her. Sure enough, the van exited right behind her and pulled up beside her in the gas station. She stepped out of her SUV and walked over to the van that was on her trail on Highway 95.

She tapped on the window, but the window seemed to be stuck at first. The person seemed to be having a problem letting the window down. Finally, the door opened; and to her surprise, it was that damn Roger.

"Why are you following me? You are stupid. You are a stupid assHole, Roger. What the fuck do you want from me?" she screamed, extremely pissed off.

"I really wasn't following you. You just happened to be in front of me," Roger replied.

"You are so ignorant, Roger. What did I see in you in the first damn place?" She turned to walk away.

"Please let's just talk, La'Roc, like humans. I need your help in defending me in a case that was brought to my attention earlier today. You are the only lawyer that can get me off," he pleaded.

"Roger, you know my phone number. Please call and set up an appointment tomorrow. I have to run. I have a life. Talk to you soon," she said as she closed the door to her Lexus and started it up.

Pulling out of the gas station and back onto the highway, she smiled to herself. *I knew that one day he would need me. What a sucker*, she thought.

A few moments later, La'Roc pulled up in her driveway, parked her SUV, jumped out, picked up Paris, and ran into the house. "Paris, are you still angry with me?" she asked as she placed him in his bed. He answered by licking the back of her hand.

"Ms. Holiday, where are you?" she called. "I need you downstairs right away, please! Ms. Holiday, will you please get Paris ready for the trip to Manhattan?"

"Okay, Ms. La'Roc. What time are we leaving?"

"We're leaving shortly. I would like to beat the traffic that is going into Manhattan."

Ms. Holiday did what was asked of her; then they all headed out the door. As she started up her car, La'Roc's cell phone rang.

"Hello, who am I speaking with?"

"Hey, baby, this is Shawn. I just called to let you know that I'm going to be a half-hour late. I should be there around seven thirty p.m., okay, Sexiful?"

"That's fine. I'm on my way to Manhattan now. So I will see you in Manhattan."

"Okay, Sexiful, drive careful."

"Ms. Holiday, is Paris okay? Don't forget to put your seat belt on and make Paris keep his seat belt on."

During the drive to Manhattan, La'Roc was thinking about what to wear tonight on her date with her young man. Traffic wasn't as bad as she thought it would be, and it was a beautiful day to take a drive.

Once she got to her condo, La'Roc helped Ms. Holiday unload the trunk, then she went upstairs to relax. She wanted to be beautiful when Shawn arrived. The condo was beautiful; Ms. Cotton had done a wonderful job on the floors, and all three bathrooms smelled of fruits. Paris ran into the master bedroom and jumped on the bed in a playful manner.

"Paris, go and get into your bed."

Paris looked at her as to say, "Please leave me alone. I am tired just like you."

She decided to give her friend Denise a call to help pass the time.

"Hello, Denise, how are you doing, girl?" she asked her friend when she picked up on the other end.

"I am good, what's up with you?"

"Nothing much, just here in Manhattan, relaxing."

"Okay. I'm assuming you're calling me to finally tell me about this new man of yours, right?" Denise asked excitedly.

"No! Not tonight, fool. I am going on a date with Shawn. I will tell you and Chantal at dinner tomorrow night, okay? Is that good enough for you?" La'Roc asked, joking with Denise.

"Of course. Will Chantal meet us there or what?"

"I will pick Chantal up after work. I'm taking her to pick up her car, which is in the shop, and we will be leaving from my condo in Manhattan. Anyway, girl, I will see you tomorrow. I will tell you everything tomorrow night at dinner." She disconnected the call after their good-byes and decided to get up and finally look for an outfit to wear for tonight.

Paris was lying in his bed as she paraded across the floor, trying to figure out what to wear. "Oh, I know what I'm going to wear, my Coach outfit," she said aloud to herself, not noticing Ms. Holiday, who was passing her bedroom door.

Her housekeeper stopped and said, "Good choice, Ms. La'Roc, you will knock him out tonight." Ms. Holiday smiled and continued to walk down the stairs.

Looking at the time, she saw that it was 5:45 p.m. It was time to take a bubble bath. Shawn was very prompt; he was always on time, which was one thing that La'Roc loved. She soaked in a Trésor bubble bath for forty-five minutes. After getting out, she did her usual routine of moisturizing her body.

She dressed in her pearl Coach slacks, a matching jacket, three-inch burnt orange heels, and bag to match. She topped off her outfit with some gorgeous accessories. She always complimented herself when she got dressed. "Damn, I look good enough to eat." She laughed out loud, and she walked out of her bedroom.

Looking at the time, it was only 6:55 p.m. It felt as if the time was slowly creeping by. She decided to have a drink while she waited for Shawn.

She mixed herself a drink and sat in her favorite chair, which was by the window, facing the Hudson River and New Jersey. She just started to sip her drink when she heard the security officer at the front gate announce over the intercom that Mr. Parker was approaching. At that moment, she started to feel very nervous. She wasn't exactly sure why. She summed it up to being that she really cared for this guy and wanted everything to be perfect, although she knew nothing was perfect, not even God.

After being let in by Ms. Holiday, Shawn walked into the sitting area. She yelled from her bedroom, "Hi, Shawn, please have a seat. I will be right with you. Mix yourself a drink if you like to."

He jokingly yelled back, "I am already sitting, and I will mix me a drink, thank you."

When she walked down the stairs from her bedroom into the hallway, she clicked on the music with her remote control. She walked into the sitting room where Shawn was waiting for her. Then she saw her man. He was looking as handsome as ever.

"Hi, Sexiful, you look beautiful. Let me take a picture. Don't move, stay right there." Shawn ran from the sitting room, out to his SUV, and ran back into the condo with a camera in his hand. "Stay right there. This is the up close shot. Sexiful, baby, you're the most beautiful woman I have ever seen. I think that I am falling in love with you all over again," he said as he prepared his camera to take her picture.

La'Roc smiled. She knew that she looked like a star, and she knew at that moment she had accomplished what she set out to do, and that was to win Shawn's love. After a few playful shots with his camera, the couple was ready to go.

"Ms. Holiday, we're leaving and don't forget to feed and give Paris his bath."

"Yes, Ms. La'Roc. I won't forget. Paris won't let me forget," Ms. Holiday laughed.

They stepped outside and walked toward Shawn's Lexus SUV. He held the door open for her. Once inside, she noticed that he had a bottle of champagne and black and red roses with a card attached.

"Baby, I want you to enjoy yourself tonight. Just be mine tonight, no other thoughts. Just think of me because I am all yours."

They drove south on 95. "Where are we going, Shawn?"

"Oh no, I'm not telling you. It's a surprise. Read the card, babe, that will give you a clue of where we are going."

She reached in the backseat and picked up the card. She turned to face Shawn and read the card aloud.

> *My dearest darling, to love you is to know you*
> *And I am beginning to know you*
> *And I love what I see in you.*
> *You are my soul mate, and*
> *I will never let you go.*
> *Just love me as I love you.*
> *I am writing this poem from*
> *My heart, and I mean*
> *Every word of what I am writing.*
> *I promise I will never hurt you*
> *Or leave you.*
> *La'Roc, I am here to stay.*
> *Love, Shawn.*
> *I hope you like it.*
> *I made this poem up.*
> *This poem is from my heart. This poem is*
> *Just for you, Sexiful.* "Let's go have dinner."

"Shawn, this is beautiful!" She leaned over and kissed him on the lips. They drove a while longer, and then pulled into Jimmy's restaurant. Shawn got out of the SUV and walked around to the passenger side. She assumed he was going to open the door for her to get out. Instead, he got inside of the SUV and opened the bottle of champagne. As they had their drink, she noticed that he looked especially good in his jeans, white shirt and a blue blazer. His shirt had three buttons open, which made him look sexy and more handsome than he already, was.

After they finished their drinks, Shawn grabbed her hand and led her from the SUV toward the restaurant, holding hands. He stopped and pulled her to him and kissed her very hard and said, "I love you, Sexiful."

The restaurant was beautiful. Shawn had rented out the entire place just for the two of them. It was very romantic.

"May I have this dance?" he asked.

She looked into his eyes and said, "Yes, you may, mister."

They shared a playful laugh as they danced to Atlantic Starr, Anthony Hampton, and many more.

After a couple of slow dances to music that Shawn had asked for personally, they sat down to order their food. They talked about families. Shawn seemed a bit uneasy.

"Listen, Sexiful, I want to tell you everything."

La'Roc ears perked up as she listened closely. "Tell me everything about what?"

Shawn looked her in the eyes. "I have a child by this girl in Queens. She moved to Boston, Massachusetts. We are not together, but we'll always have a connection because of the child. I don't love her. I love you, and I want you and me to be together forever. Baby, I need you."

"Tonight, let's just enjoy each other, Shawn."

A waiter came over to check on the couple. They ordered a bottle of white wine, and Shawn wanted some crab sticks. La'Roc declined. He started to tease her. "Watching your weight?"

"No," she insisted.

"Good. Right because you don't have to worry about your weight. You are just fine the way you are. I love what I see. Don't change a thing. Sexiful, you are the entire woman that I need, and you are the woman that I want to be with."

Finally, their dinner arrived. La'Roc had red snapper with green salad. Shawn ordered blue fish with baked potato and green salad. They drank the white wine. The band played their favorite tunes, and after finishing their meals, they danced in each other's arms most of the night. Shawn held her tightly in his arms; it was hard for her to breathe. She didn't care; she was with the man that she loved at that moment. When she was with Shawn, he made her feel like a high school girl in love for the first time.

As the last song played, they laughed and began to put on their jackets. Suddenly, Shawn picked her up and started kissing her with tears running down his cheeks. Shawn looked at her. "I'm sorry, babe, for crying, but I have never been with a woman like you before. The feeling I have for you is unexplainable. I never had this feeling about any other woman like I have for you. I love you, Sexiful. The tears I cry are happy tears, and they are all for you, baby."

La'Roc smiled and planted another kiss on his lips as she wiped away his tears. "You're so sweet," she said.

As they left the restaurant and walked toward Shawn's SUV, he gripped her hand so tight she thought he was going to fracture her wrist.

Shawn walked to the passenger side and opened the door for her. As she sat down on the seat, Shawn buckled her seat belt. She looked into his eyes; there was so much love and sadness. She kissed him. "Baby, what's wrong?" he asked.

"I love you too, Shawn, but I think we should slow down just a little until you take care of your unfinished business with your son's mother."

"Sexiful, there is nothing going on between my son's mother and me. Please believe me."

"Shawn, I have a feeling that Missis has an agenda and you are a part of that plan. I know how we women think since I am a woman. I know these things."

"Baby, we have been broken up for almost a year now. She has moved on with her life, and I have moved on with mine. Let's not ruin this night talking about something that's not important to me. Baby, you are the one that is important to me tonight and all the other nights if you'll allow me to be in your life. Sexiful, you have nothing to worry about. I am yours."

Still feeling a bit uneasy, La'Roc managed to say, "Okay, Shawn, we will not talk about Misses tonight, but we will be discussing it sooner than you think. Tonight you just tell me how beautiful I look." She smiled to herself.

The drive home was silent as they held hands. La'Roc was practically sitting in his seat as he drove her home.

"Shawn, I really enjoyed myself tonight. It was a pleasure being with you." He squeezed her hand just a little bit tighter in response.

After pulling into her garage, she looked at Shawn. He looked so damn handsome in his jeans, white shirt, and blue blazer, she thought. "Shawn, baby, it was very thoughtful of you to rent out the entire restaurant just for me. I don't understand how you could afford it."

"Baby, didn't I tell you that I owned a realty company?"

That had completely slipped her mind. "Oh, sweetheart, I forgot, I'm sorry. You see, sometimes I don't pay attention, my bad." She smiled, but she felt really bad. She pulled his hand to her lips and kissed his hand, then began putting his fingers into her mouth, sucking them one by one. Shawn had a smile on his face that stretched from one ear to the other.

He got out of the SUV and walked around to the passenger side and opened the door. He reached for her hand with that beautiful smile and helped her out. He carried her inside of the condo, up the stairs to her master bedroom, and laid her gently on her bed. He then pulled a chair away from her makeup room and put it near her bed and placed his head on her chest. "Shawn, sweetheart, the night was great."

"Baby, it is always great being with you."

"Let's have a drink and go soak in the whirlpool," La'Roc suggested. "That sounds great!" He got up and walked out of the bedroom toward the bar area. "Oh, babe, I forget to ask you, what you are drinking?" he asked. She yelled back to him, "Cream of casket would be nice."

"I think I can love that guy," she said to herself as she slipped into the whirlpool fully dressed.

Shawn walked back into the room with two glasses in his big hands. He handed over hers, and they toasted to their first real date.

Shawn placed his drink on a coaster by the whirlpool. As she sipped her drink, he slipped her clothes off and kissed her body all over from head to toe. *This man knows how to make love*, she thought. He was by far the best lover she had ever had. And he was all hers for now.

After soaking in the whirlpool, they dried each other off. La'Roc ran into the bedroom. Shawn chased behind her. They laughed and played. Their noise must have awakened Paris from his sleep because he woke up with what seemed to be an attitude. He began barking at Shawn like he was holding a conversation with him. Paris seemed to be saying, "Get the hell out of here, and let me get some damn sleep."

La'Roc smiled. "Okay, boy." She slipped on her Versace robe and walked Paris to his room and put him to bed. Paris had a big room with all dog furniture. In his room, he had two walk-in closets with all his clothes hanging up on clothes hangers.

She returned to the bedroom. "Hi, baby, you missed me?" she asked, smiling.

"Of course I missed you. Did you get Paris to bed?"

"Yes, hopefully he will stay in his room."

They both laughed. She gave Shawn a bottle of moisturizer so he could moisturize her body. He reached for the bottle that she held in her hand and started to rub her legs first and between her legs, her thighs, her stomach, and her back. Now it was her turn to moisturize his body. First, she played a game with him. The game she played was rubbing ice on his back, up and down his spine, in between his legs, into his groin area, and down his legs. As she played her X-rated game, she looked at him. She knew she had him right where she wanted him—in the palm of her hands.

Making love that night was more exciting than the first night. He was so gentle and loving she didn't want him to stop. That night,

Shawn made love to her entire body, from head to toe. He took her to a place where she had never been before. He made her feel as if she was the only person in the world. She felt as though she was in heaven with God's angels.

They cuddled for a few minutes after their lovemaking. Then she felt him easing out from under her arms. He was getting out of the bed. She didn't want him to leave, but she knew in her heart it was time for him to go.

Shawn took a shower and kissed her good-bye. He said, "I love you. See you later." She kissed him as he walked out the door.

She sat on the edge of her bed for a moment and thought about the lovemaking that they had shared the previous night. She began to daydream but thought it best to cut it short. She knew that she had to get ready to prepare for her case the next day. She got out of bed and walked into the bathroom to take a shower. Shawn had left her burning up inside and wanting more of him. She could feel his strong arms wrap around her body and his strong body rubbing against hers. When they showered together, she played with his six-packs. Playing with his six-packs turned him on, and she like it when he was turned on because when he was turned on, it turned her on.

Stepping out of the tub, she ran into the master room before Paris could see her. But the little devil beat her to the room. Paris was sitting in her makeup chair, looking out the window, pretending that he was not in the room. "Paris, you have another attitude? I wish the hell you could talk, maybe you wouldn't continue to get those little dog attitudes. Paris, go to your room now!"

Paris got down from the chair and went over to her and licked her hand. Melting instantly, La'Roc gave in. "Okay, mommy forgives you, but I can not play with you tonight. Mommy, have too pick out an outfit to ware to work tomorrow." You need a playmate. Would you like that?" She grabbed her loyal companion, and they cuddled in bed and fell asleep.

The next morning, she awoke to the sound of her ringing alarm. The outfit she chose for her appearance in court was a pea green jacket and matching skirt and her three-inch green Babe heels. She grabbed her Louis Vuitton shoulder bag, gold belt, and gold accessories. For the life of her, she could not decide what to do with her hair. She finally decided to wear it down.

"Ms. Holiday, please place my laptop and presentation in my briefcase. Thank you."

"Okay, Ms. La'Roc. I put your breakfast on the table. I will take Paris to the park after I go shopping. Paris also has an appointment today at the vet for his yearly checkup."

"Okay, I'm bringing home a playmate for Paris today. How does that sound?" La'Roc asked her housekeeper.

"That would be great!" Ms. Holiday answered, sounding excited. "That would be great. Maybe he will change his attitude," she laughed.

La'Roc decided to do her seven-mile morning walk. She was feeling exceptionally good this morning. When she returned from her walk, she did a few Pilates scratches and took a quick shower, then got ready for work to go win her case.

Before she walked out the door, Ms. Holiday stopped her and gave her a glass of orange juice. She walked to her Lexus, got in, and started the car up. She threw on her sunglasses and drove out of the gate. As she drove, she saw Roger's car behind her. She stopped her Lexus and exited her car. She walked over to Roger, who had also pulled over.

"What is it now?"

"Are you going to represent me in court?" he asked.

"Roger, can you find another lawyer?"

"No. I want you. I want the best, and that is you."

Rolling her eyes, she gave in. "I'm on my way to court now. Meet me at my office about five."

"Okay, I will see you at five," Roger said as La'Roc walked away.

She got in her car and pulled off in a hurry. She was driving eighty miles per hour. She laughed out loud. "I knew he would say it one day that I was the best." Now she had to save that crazy man. She thought back to when she first met Roger. He was extremely nice to her and was very helpful when she was starting her career. She smiled and concluded that she didn't mind saving his ass.

Driving into Manhattan was a bitch. Traffic was up the ass. It was a mess. She thought of a way to pass the time. She turned on her car radio and popped in a CD. The first song that blared through her speakers was "Can You Feel Me?" by Anthony Hamilton. She smiled to herself, thinking that was one of Shawn's favorite songs after "Send for Me" by Atlantic Starr. She was beginning to get hot although her window was all the way down. Her hair was not blowing in the wind as she was driving at a slow speed due to the damn traffic out there. Sitting, stuck in traffic, she listened to her music and thought about Shawn and the way he made love to her the previous night. After a while, the traffic seemed to let up. She changed lanes and hit the gas. She glanced at the time on the radio's clock. She was running late.

"Move your damn car, fool! Stupid ass man can't drive for shit!"

Maneuvering her Lexus in and out of the traffic lanes, she finally cleared the traffic. She was able to speed like she wanted to. Her hair was blowing as she drove eighty miles per hour. She loved driving fast and the feeling of the wind blowing in her face.

"We are almost there, baby," she said to herself. Her cell phone started to ring. She quickly looked at the screen. It was Shawn. She pressed the Answer button on her Bluetooth headset.

"Hello, handsome. How is it going today, babe?"

"Hi, baby, I just wanted to hear your sweet voice."

"I needed to hear your voice too, babe. I'm going to have a rough day today in court. Baby, do you recall the case I told you about the hit and run? That is my job for today, and this is one hell of a case.

I have my work cut out for me today. Baby, did I tell you that I have a meeting with Roger today after work. Remember Roger is my ex."

"Why do you have to meet up with this guy, baby?"

"Roger has a case against him coming up, and he wants me to defend him. Because I am the best! Ha-ha," she joked.

"Baby, please, be careful. We're still on for tonight, right?" Shawn asked. "Yes, we are. Nothing can stop you and I from being together tonight. I'm at the courthouse now. So I'll call you when I'm done." She disconnected their phone call and parked the Lexus.

She opened the car door and stretched her long legs out the door. She gathered up her laptop and briefcase and headed up the courthouse steps in style.

She greeted her colleagues with a smile as she passed them and continued to part C-5 where she would be defending her client.

"Hey, La'Roc, you're looking good as always."

"Thanks, Kim, for the compliment. Have you talked to Curtis today?"

"No, I haven't talked to him today," Kim responded.

"If you see him, tell him that I need to see him right away. He is a witness in this case. I need him pronto." Kim nodded her head in agreement, and La'Roc walked into the courtroom, and all eyes were on her.

"Good morning, Mr. District Attorney," she spoke.

"Hi, Ms. Rose. Are you ready for me today?" the district attorney, Mr. Stable, asked.

"Yes, I am Mr. DA." He smiled and walked over to his table in the courtroom.

The court officer belted out the case number, and then asked for all parties to rise. He introduced the honorable Judge Perkins. After the judge entered and took his seat, the court officer instructed everyone else to be seated. Judge Perkins recited the basic facts of the case in open court.

"Will the defendant please rise." La'Roc stood up along with her client, Mr. Robertson.

The judge spoke, "Mr. Robertson, you are being charged with leaving the scene of an accident. You are also being sued by the victim for lost wages and pain and suffering. You have entered a plea of not guilty. Is this correct?"

"Yes, it is, Your Honor," Mr. Robertson answered.

"Very well then. Ms. Rose, you may call your first witness."

Mr. Robertson sat down.

"Thank you, Your Honor," La'Roc said. "I would like to call Mr. Charles Boston to the stand."

The court officer, who was standing by the doors in the rear of the courtroom, opened the door and beckoned for someone to come to the room. La'Roc turned and faced the rear of the room. A short dark bald man with a cane entered. He took his seat on the witness stand. After being sworn in by the court officer, La'Roc walked over to him.

"Please state your name for the record," she said.

The man answered, "My name is Charles D. Boston."

"Mr. Boston, on the night of May 20, 2009, you made a statement, and in your statement, you stated that you witnessed a man jumping from a car, running down the street, yelling, and I quote, 'I just ran over something about ten blocks back, and I think it is hurt real bad. Please help me somebody.' Do you recall giving that statement to an officer?"

"Yes. I do recall."

"Do you see that man that was running away from you in the courtroom today?"

Mr. Boston scanned the room with his eyes and stopped on Mr. Robertson. "I think it's him," he said, pointing at the defendant.

"You think it was the defendant? If he was running away from you, how did you make a positive identification, Mr. Boston?" He appeared nervous and hesitant. "Mr. Boston, please answer the question," La'Roc pressed on.

"I'm sure he was tall like him, but now I can't be for certain. I don't want to perjure myself, to be honest with you. I am sorry."

La'Roc smirked. "We appreciate your honesty. No more questions for this witness, Your Honor." She glanced over toward the DA's table. Mr. Perkins shook his head. "Your witness," La'Roc said. He refused the opportunity to question Mr. Boston.

Preparing herself to call her next witness, she heard the courtroom doors open and shut. In rolled the victim, Mr. Martin, on a wheelchair. He was sporting a neck brace, left arm in a sling. La'Roc shook her head, thinking to herself, *Oh my goodness, what we have here?* As he situated himself by the DA, they whispered. La'Roc stood up from her place behind her table.

"Your Honor, I would like to introduce into evidence Exhibit A." She carried two folders in her hand, one of which she handed to the judge.

"Your Honor, the people were not made aware of such evidence," Mr. Stable said.

La'Roc walked over to his table and plopped down the other folder. Mr. Stable sighed, knowing that whatever the folder contained would not be beneficial to his case.

"Your Honor, the people request a fifteen-minute recess to go over the new evidence."

"Granted," the judge said.

La'Roc went to her table and sat beside her client. They smiled, knowing that the case would be over in a matter of moments. The folder that she gave to the judge and Mr. Stable had pictures of Mr. Martin lifting and moving furniture as well as giving a child a piggyback ride. She watched and waited for both the DA and Mr. Martin's reaction when they found out they had no case.

"May we approach the bench, Your Honor?" she asked. "I have all the evidence that I need to have your client arrested for filing a false claim. Would you like to continue this trial?" La'Roc asked.

"Let's discuss this in the chambers," the judge suggested.

After the two lawyers chatted with each other, Mr. Stable decided it will be best if his client were to drop the charges and the case would be dismissed. La'Roc couldn't have agreed more. She smiled and walked back into the courtroom. The judge announced that the case Mr. Martin brought against Mr. Robertson was being dismissed. "But as for the charge of leaving the scene of an accident, Mr. Robertson, I'm sentencing you to thirty days in jail."

Before he was done, he gave Mr. Martin a long lecture about the law and the potential consequences of lying. Mr. Martin held his head down in shame and apologized to the court and Mr. Robertson.

Wow! What a day, La'Roc thought as she walked out of the courtroom. The judge called her into his chambers and congratulated her on a good case well done in court. "Keep up the work, Ms. Rose. You may have to represent me one day," he smiled.

On her way out, every lawyer that she passed congratulated her on her victory. She knew that she was good, so why not accept the compliments? It wasn't every day that a defense attorney got over on the prosecution.

Getting into her car, her neck seemed to be tense. "I know I need a massage," she said aloud. Starting up her Lexus, she put on her sunglasses and combed out her hair. She turned on her radio and pressed Play on the CD player. She was on her way to meet with Roger. She pulled out her cell to call Shawn. She needed to hear his sexy voice. She was dialing his number when she looked into the rearview mirror. Shawn was right behind her in his work van. *"She pulled her car over to the curb and turned off her car initiation."* He got out of his van and walked over to her car. "Hello, babe, I missed you today. How was your day?" he asked after planting a kiss on her lips.

"Well, I won the case. That is one good thing. And another good thing just happened."

"What's that, babe?"

She smiled. "You are behind me protecting me."

"You need protection?"

"Yes. Are you protecting me from the bad guys?" They both began to laugh.

"Sexiful, stop playing. Turn off the car."

"Oh, baby, you want little old me to get out of the car? Maybe I need protection from you." She shut off the car, and he joined her for about thirty minutes before she reminded him she had an appointment with Roger. La'Roc didn't let anything interfere with her work.

"Hey, Sexiful, are we still on for tonight? I am just checking."

"Yes, handsome, I will call you as soon as I get home, okay. Talk to you later. I have to meet Roger in about fifteen minutes."

He kissed her a few times, and they went their separate ways.

The drive to her office was short and smooth. When she pulled up, Roger was waiting for her in his car. She ran into her office to get settled in and to get started on his case. She was not looking to go to court with this case. From what she can gather, it was an open-and-shut case. In the event that it did go to trial, she was planning on giving the case to a lawyer that she trusted. She knew that Roger would be angry, but he was always angry about something.

She called for Roger to come inside. He walked in with a long face.

"Hi, Mr. Roger Spring, have a seat."

"Thanks," he said, sounding gloomy.

"So let's discuss the case. Let me tell you from the beginning, if this case goes to trial, I will appoint you another lawyer that I trust, and I will be with him every step of the way. I will be there as his consultant. Roger, you have nothing to worry about. Tell me what's going on, and how did you get mixed up in this shit that has you needing a lawyer. I hope you can understand why I can't defend you."

"Yes, I understand."

"Okay, let's get on with it. What brought you to my office today? Roger, please tell me the truth. I know when you are being dishonest, Mr. Spring."

"Well, here goes," he started. "I was dating this female about nine months ago. I didn't know that she was using my car to transport illegal drugs into the city from New Jersey. I swear I had nothing to do with that shit."

"Mr. Spring, respect me in my office. I will not allow that type of language in my place of work."

"I'm sorry. I'm just so angry right now."

"Well, it will be all right, I promise you, as long as you're telling me the truth. I will get you off, and there will be no trial. I will set up an appointment for a conference meeting with her lawyer. How did you find out about the drugs being transported back and forth?"

"She was arrested last Friday, and the internal affairs met with me on Saturday. I was told at that point to get a lawyer—not just any lawyer, get the best. That is why I am here."

"Have you discussed this case with anyone else.?" she asked.

"No La'Roc, I have not discussed this case with anyone. La' Roc, Thank you Ms Rose.

"Good. Mr. Spring, we will have you cleared in no time if nothing comes up. I just hope that she is not trying to build a case against you. You think she will do something like that?"

"I will tell you the truth. I don't know. I didn't think that she would do what she did. I don't put anything past her now."

"Roger, call me later on in the week. I will introduce you to the lawyer that will be handling your case. His name is Alex Power. He is a damn good lawyer. We will take good care of you. Don't worry. We'll talk more about it after you meet Mr. Power."

He smiled and extended his arms for a hug. She grabbed one of his hands and shook it firmly. She was going to keep this case with Roger on a strictly business level.

As she walked out her office to her car, she could see someone walking toward her.

"May I help you?" she asked.

"My name is Mrs. Sanchez. You don't know me, but I was referred to you by my brother-in-law Jose and my husband." She extended her hand for a handshake. La'Roc obliged. Mrs. Sanchez continued, "My husband needs a good lawyer, and he said that you were the best. My husband has been in prison for a crime he didn't commit. He isn't guilty, please help us."

"Mrs. Sanchez, here is my business card," she said as she dug around her purse for her card. When she found one, she handed it to the woman. "I would like to speak to your husband. Tell him to give me a call."

"He is in a prison upstate. It's called Riverton. Ms. Rose, my husband is a well-known and respected police officer. He was decorated three times for his bravery."

"Tell him to contact me tomorrow. I'm not promising you that I will take his case. If necessary, I will appoint another lawyer to take the case."

"Ms. Rose, he wants you," Mrs. Sanchez said, cutting her short. She gave La'Roc the information that she needed to contact her and her husband. As she handed La'Roc the information, she pleaded with her eyes.

La'Roc took the paper and placed it in her briefcase. "I'll see what I can do, Mrs. Sanchez."

Mrs. Sanchez was a short stocky woman who seemed to be in her late forties. Her face showed lines of uncertainties and concern for her husband being in prison. La'Roc knew it was never easy for a police officer on the other side of the jail bars.

"Good night, Mrs. Sanchez, I will call you tomorrow."

"Thank you, Ms. Rose, and God bless you."

Mrs. Sanchez turned and walked away, and La'Roc got into her Lexus.

Getting into her car, she looked down at her wristwatch. "Damn, I'm running late." As she picked up her cell phone, it started to ring. It was Shawn.

"Hey, baby, are you all right? I am beginning to worry about you, Where are you?" he asked after she picked up her cell.

"Sweetheart, I'm on my way home. I'm sorry, baby. I got caught up in a new case that I'm considering taking. I will talk to you as soon as I get home, okay, handsome. Where are you?"

"I'm right behind you, baby." She looked in her rearview, and Shawn was on her bumper with that beautiful smile that she loved so much. She smiled.

"Love you, baby, I will see you at the condo." She hung up and headed to the condo with Shawn on her tail, her radio playing his favorite song.

Pulling into her garage with Shawn following closely behind her in his SUV made her feel like the richest woman in the world. She felt lucky to have a man like Shawn. He parked his Lexus and walked over to hers. He opened her door, reached inside, and kissed her as hard as he could.

"I missed you today, baby. Don't ever go for a whole day without calling me again when you are meeting with someone like Roger. Especially your ex. Promise me that, okay?" He smiled. La'Roc promised.

Shawn picked her up and carried her into the house. As they entered the den, Paris ran down the stairs and jumped all over them. They both fell on the floor, laughing and playing with Paris. Ms. Holiday ran from the kitchen.

"What's going on out here? Paris, come over here."

"Ms. Holiday, it's okay. Paris just missed his mother and father. I didn't get a chance to pick up his playmate today. I was overwhelmed with work."

"Yes, maybe you and Mr. Shawn will be able to get some rest," Ms. Holiday joked.

"Did Chantal or Denise call? Remember, it is girls' night out tomorrow."

"Yes, they both called. The messages are on the answering machine." La'Roc followed Ms. Holiday out of the den so that she could listen to the messages. Both of her friends called to confirm that they were still on for dinner the following night. When she returned to the den, she saw that Shawn had fallen asleep on the floor. He was tired after working at his two jobs. The very thick carpet on her floors made Shawn more than comfortable. She left the den and decided to call Chantal, Denise, and her mother. She took a quick shower and joined Shawn on the den floor. She didn't realize that she was tired until she hit the floor next to him.

No lovemaking, just sleep for the first time since she and Shawn met.

Waking up the following morning in Shawn's arms, she felt like a queen and he was her king. Shawn kissed her good morning and went upstairs to take a shower before leaving for work. Ms. Holiday called Shawn for breakfast, and La'Roc went upstairs to start her exercise before taking a shower. After Shawn finished his breakfast, he came upstairs to kiss her good-bye before leaving for work. He walked out the door, and she continued with her exercise.

After her workout, she went downstairs for breakfast.

While eating, she decided to make some phone calls. She called her mother, sister, and daughter and invited them to lunch and a day out for shopping.

She walked Paris around for a while and decided to take a quick trip to pick up his playmate while she had the time. When she brought the newest addition home, Ms. Holiday was happy. They decided to call him Biscuit. Paris played shy at first. Ms. Holiday suggested holding both puppies in her lap would force them to interact. When she did, they seemed to respond a little better to each other. Paris was trying to lick Biscuit as if to introduce himself to his brother. "The job is done, Ms. Holiday. Paris has a friend!" They both laughed.

After sitting with the puppies for a while, La'Roc decided it was time to take a shower and get dressed. After showering, she sat on the edge of the bed with her briefcase. She decided to call Alex, the attorney she wanted to work with her on the Sanchez case. "Hello, sweetie, how's it going?"

"Hey, miss, you want something?" Alex joked.

"How did you know? I need to talk to you about a case that I'm interested in."

"I'm all ears," Alex said.

She informed him of the conversation that she had with Mrs. Sanchez about defending her husband. "Are you free tomorrow afternoon between one and three? I want you to take a ride with me upstate."

"Why, what's up?"

"I'll tell on the way to the prison."

"What prison?"

She laughed. "Mr. Attorney, you ask too many questions. We will talk tomorrow. You will love it, trust me. See you soon."

After speaking to Alex, she got dressed. She wore olive green jeans, a button-up blouse, and a green jacket to match her jeans. She mixed a drink and just relaxed for a while as she waited for the time to go shopping with her family. She lounged in her comfortable chair by the window until 2:30 p.m. It was time to pick up her mother. Although La'Roc gave her a truck as well as a car, she didn't want her mother driving today.

"Ms. Holiday, I'm going out with my family for a while. I'll be back shortly." She talked to Paris and Biscuit briefly, and then headed for the door. "Ms. Holiday," she yelled, "why don't you take your babies to the park and let them run you crazy." They both laughed.

Walking in the garage, she decided to take her BMW. She put on her sunglasses and headed for the FDR. She had to go to Westchester to pick up her mother. She dialed her daughter first to let her know that she was en route. There was no answer. She picked up her cell to call her sister to let her know that she was on her way. "Please call your niece and have her meet us at the restaurant. Lord knows, that child never picks up when you call her phone." Her sister said she would.

La'Roc picked up her mother and headed for the restaurant in lower Manhattan. Looking at the time on the clock radio, she was running late. "Okay, Mom, hold on, we have to move!"

La'Roc pulled up into the valet parking section of the restaurant. She got out and walked over to the other side of the car. "Come on, Mom. Let's go."

As she helped her mother get out of the car, her phone began to ring. She looked at the screen.

"Hello, handsome, what's up?" she said to Shawn when she answered. "You are. How're you, babe?"

"I'm good, Shawn. I'm having lunch with my family now. Then after lunch, we're going on a shopping trip. By the way, I need you to go someplace with me tonight. I want you to meet my daughter, sister, mother, and my grandson. I will call with all the details later." She hung up the phone, and she and her mother walked into the restaurant, holding hands and laughing.

Her sister and daughter were already in the restaurant, waiting for them, having a glass of white wine.

They joined them at the table. The waiter came over to the table to check on them. La'Roc and her mother ordered a glass of red wine. They all decided to have salad and seafood platters. Lunch was great. The family talked, laughed, and reminisced. After finishing their meals, the group left the restaurant, laughing at everything and everybody.

La'Roc and her mother got back into her BMW; L'Oreal and Courtney got into their cars. They decided to meet each other by Fifty-ninth and Columbus Circle to start their shopping trip. La'Roc's daughter and grandson had a modeling event on *The Tonight Show* at Madison Square Garden. That was where she planned to introduce Shawn to her family. The ride to the shopping area was nice. La'Roc was enjoying herself. *This is the only time I can really be myself. When I am with my family, I can relax. They make me laugh*, she thought.

The women had a blast shopping. They shopped at stores like Bloomingdales, Sapphire, Babe, New York & Company, and Sacks Fifth Avenue. After shopping, La'Roc and her mother decided to get dressed at her condominium in Manhattan.

As they pulled up at La'Roc's condominium, Paris and Biscuit ran down the stairs to greet her. She picked up both of her babies, held them in her arms, and ran up the stairs.

"Ms. Holiday, please help my mother with her bath and getting dressed for the fashion show tonight. Are you coming with us tonight to see my daughter walk down the runway?" she asked.

"Yes, I will be there with bells on. I wouldn't miss it for world!" Ms. Holiday exclaimed.

La'Roc decided to call Shawn to make sure that he was still able to make the night in question.

"Hello, Mr. Parker, are you ready for my surprise tonight?" she asked when he answered the phone.

"Hi, Sexiful. Yes, I'm looking forward to it. What should I wear to this surprise gathering?"

"I'm wearing a soft yellow gown."

"Okay, I will wear my green suit, light green shirt, and yellow tie with little green background. Is that okay with you?"

"Yes, babe, that sounds like a plan to me. Just wear something to make me look beautiful." They both laughed.

"See you soon, Sexiful."

She smiled as she walked over to her nightstand. Already knowing what she wanted to wear, she decided to get into the Jacuzzi with a drink of Nuvo.

While pouring her drink, she asked her mother if she would like something.

"Of course, La'Roc, pour me a glass of white wine, okay, baby," she answered from the other bathroom.

"Okay, Ms. Lady." She smiled as she mixed her mother a drink. She was so excited for her family to meet Shawn. She couldn't wait to see their faces. She knew they would like him. He's just that kind of guy. He was a charmer, and he was very respectful. He was tall, handsome, light brown complexion; and she liked all of that. La'Roc looked at her mother and thought to herself that her mother was cool even at the age of seventy-five. She knew that her mother wouldn't mind the difference in their ages. Her mother was happy as long as her children were happy.

Her mother must have been reading her mind. She appeared at the doorway. "La'Roc, when am I going to meet that good-looking man I keep hearing about? Chantal told me you had a new man in your life. Baby, I'm happy for you, and he better be good to my big-time lawyer." She came over and kissed her daughter on her forehead. "I love you, baby. I'm so proud of what you have accomplished, and you did it all by yourself. La'Roc, you are strong. I remember when we didn't have food on the table and you would always say, 'Mommy, we will be all right, I promise,' and baby, look at you now."

"Mommy, we did it together. If it wasn't for you, I wouldn't have made it by myself. You and Daddy were always there when I wasn't able to get up in the morning, or Dad would give me his last dime to get some cookies or a piece of candy. He would say, 'Baby, this will help you to get through the morning, and we will worry about tomorrow when tomorrow comes.' Mommy, I miss him so much." Tears welled in her eyes as she thought about her father. La'Roc's father was killed in a car accident when she was in her freshman year of college. He was a very good husband and a good father. He worked two jobs to try to give his children everything that they needed. She would always love and remember him as being a good father and a good husband.

When she got the call that her father was killed, she thought she would just crawl up in a corner and die, but she knew that her mother and siblings needed her to be strong. She called for flight reservations and headed for South Carolina. It was a very sad funeral, but he was well loved by all. The church was packed with families, relatives, and friends. After the funeral, she left and headed back to Howard University. That day, she promised her mother that she would never have to worry about anything ever again. She kept that promise. Her mother is very well-off; La'Roc made sure of that. She had everything she needed and everything she ever wanted. The same thing went for her siblings. She gave them their start in their own businesses. Two of her brothers took the money and ran and made bad investments. But she didn't have time to dwell on that.

"La'Roc, you okay, honey?" her mother asked. Concern marked her face. "Yeah, Mom, I am fine. I was just thinking about something. I'm going to go relax a little before it's time to get ready." Her mother rubbed her back and headed out of the room. La'Roc stepped into the Jacuzzi with her drink and played her R. Kelly CD.

After about thirty minutes of soaking, La'Roc got out of the Jacuzzi and sat on her bed. "Ms. Holiday, please get my sister and daughter on the phone. Then take Paris and Biscuit to their playroom, okay? Thanks."

"Okay, Ms. Rose."

La'Roc decided to go into Paris and Biscuit's playroom. Paris jumped up on her. Biscuit seemed to be thinking "Come here, Biscuit. I love you too." He ran full force and leapt on her lap. Biscuit seemed as if he was waiting for his clue to be a part of the family. Ms. Holiday stood in the doorway and watched with a smile on her face.

"Ms. Holiday, did you get my sister or my daughter on the phone yet?"

"I'm going to get them on the phone now. I just wanted to tell you Chantal and Denise called and stated that they will meet you at the show tonight. Denise said that she will be riding with Chantal. They wanted to know what to wear, and I told them that you were wearing a gown. I hope I wasn't out of line."

"No, you weren't out of line, Ms. Holiday. Thanks for telling them."

Ms. Holiday exited the room and reappeared moments later with the cordless phone in hand. "Ms. Rose, your sister and daughter are on the phone," she said from the doorway.

"Thank you. You can just inform my daughter that her driver will pick her and my grandson up at seven thirty. Inform my sister to meet the driver downstairs at eight thirty, and we will meet in front of the garden at nine o'clock. I have the tickets. Shawn will be riding with me and Mommy."

Ms. Holiday forwarded the messages, and then hung up. She left the room and walked back to the other room where La'Roc's mother was waiting for her.

La'Roc headed over to her closet where her gown was hanging up. She took it down gently and admired it. It was her first time wearing her Versace gown. She put it on, and it fit her frame nice and snug. She looked at herself in the mirror and smiled. Ms. Holiday appeared in the doorway. "Mom is ready, and she looks beautiful. Maybe she will model tonight, huh?" she laughed.

The doorbell rang. Ms. Holiday went to open it and let Shawn in. He walked to the back room where La'Roc was. *Oh my god, he looks so damn good. He should have been arrested. It should be a crime for someone to be looking that damn good*, La'Roc thought to herself. His green tailor-made tux—it matched her yellow gown and four-inch green heels perfectly.

"Sexiful, baby, you look fantastic as always."

"Baby, you look so damn handsome in your tux. The colors look great on you, sweetheart."

He blushed.

"I want you to meet someone," La'Roc said. She grabbed him by the hand and led him down the hall to the room where her mother was putting the final touches on her hair. "Mom," La'Roc called. Her mother turned around, and a smile spread across her face as she looked Shawn up and down. "This is Shawn Parker. He is a special friend of mine. Shawn, this is my mother, Geneva."

Shawn walked over to Geneva and extended his and as she grabbed his hand to shake. "The pleasure is all mines."

Sensing that Shawn had received her mother's approval, she asked if everyone was ready. They all agreed. Ms. Holiday put out more food for the puppies; then they were on their way. They all walked out to the limo, looking as good as hell. Shawn and La'Roc walked out hand in hand. Geneva and Ms. Holiday followed closely behind.

The ride was smooth; they talked the whole ride. When they got to Madison Square Garden, where the show was being held, Shawn kissed La'Roc and said, "I love you."

"Please, Shawn, I know that you love me, and I love you. We are going to have a good time tonight. Let's go have some fun!"

After handing over their tickets, the group entered. La'Roc asked Shawn to escort her mother and Ms. Holiday to their seats. "I will join you in a few minutes. I must see my daughter and grandson before the show starts. I have a present to give them." She couldn't wait to see the surprise on Shawn and her mother's face when her daughter and grandson walked down the runway.

After a bit of searching, she found her daughter's dressing room. She entered and gave her a kiss and a small gift box. Courtney opened the box and found a set of car keys to a BMW. She started to cry. "Mommy, Mommy, I love you! Thank you so much." She jumped up and down and hugged her mother as tight as she could.

"Baby, please let go," La'Roc laughed. "I need to see my grandson before the show starts." She walked down the hall to her grandson's dressing room. When she found it, she knocked and entered; he was shocked.

"Hi, Grandma, are you looking for me?" They both laughed and hugged each other. When they let go, La'Roc handed him a small gift box identical to the one she had given her daughter. He opened it. "Oh, wow, is this for me?" His eyes opened wide.

"Yes, baby, because you are my little man, right?" He pulled out a set of keys to his new Acura SUV. He hugged his grandmother tight.

"Thanks, Grandma, I love you."

She wished him good luck and walked away smiling. She made her way to where her family was seated. They had some of the best of seats in the place.

Shawn greeted her with a smile. "Hey, babe, everything okay?" She smiled. "Yes, everything is just fine."

Moments later, after La'Roc returned to her seat, the show was getting ready to start. La'Roc began to get butterflies in her stomach. She couldn't wait to see the expression on her mother's face. She wanted to show off her daughter and grandson to Shawn. They were her pride and joy. "Are you guys ready for the big surprise? Here it is, get ready!"

The music started, and La'Roc saw her grandson about to walk down the runway. Seeing him walk down that runway made her so proud; she felt as if she would faint.

Her mother's mouth was wide-open. She was so shocked to see them walk down the runway. La'Roc leaned in close to Shawn as Courtney strutted her stuff down the runway, looking as beautiful as ever. "Shawn, that's my grandson and my daughter up there."

Shawn looked at her. "Sexiful, why didn't you tell me that picture in your living room was your daughter and your grandson."

"Well, sweetie, you didn't ask me," she said, smiling as she looked at her grandson. Her mother was trying to talk with tears of happiness running down her face.

The show was fantastic. Her daughter and grandson stole the spotlight. They were, by far, the best models to walk down that runway. Afterward, they joined the rest of their family. They were greeted with a bunch of hugs and congratulations. They both were happy about the gifts that they had received from La'Roc. They bragged to La'Roc's mom.

Her grandson said, "I got a new SUV."

Her daughter said, "I have the new BMW that I always wanted. Thanks, Mommy."

La'Roc smiled. "You will not be able to pick it up until tomorrow because I'm having them customize to your taste." That made them even more excited. After the excitement died down, La'Roc introduced her daughter and grandson to Shawn. They exchanged greetings. And Shawn congratulated them on a wonderful show.

"Group hugs, everybody. That includes you, Mr. Shawn," Courtney said. They all smiled and hugged each other. La'Roc was smiling because she was happy that everyone approved of Shawn. Her family's approval was very important to her. They all seemed to like him, which made her love him even more.

"She won't answer you when she is with Shawn unless you call her Sexiful," she heard someone say. She turned around, and it was her two best friends, Chantal and Denise. They had come to the show, but weren't able to get seats close to where La'Roc and her family had been sitting.

"Hey, girls, what's up?" she asked.

"We were looking for you all night."

Denise and Chantal congratulated La'Roc's daughter and grandson. Afterward, they went to Geneva and kissed and hugged her for a few minutes.

Shawn's mouth was still open; he couldn't believe that La'Roc's daughter was a doctor and a model. He was also surprised to know that her grandson was a model and an actor. He was a top-paid model and had small roles in the best of movies with some of the best actors.

Courtney just got out of medical school and decided to take off for a while. She graduated top of her class.

Shawn complimented them both and gave Courtney a hug and slapped five to La'Roc's grandson's hand and wished them both luck in their careers.

La'Roc phoned the drivers and asked them to meet everyone outside of Madison Square Garden. "Chantal, who are you and Denise riding with?" she asked her friend.

"I am riding with Denise, Ms. Sexiful Rose," Chantal answered.

La'Roc blushed, and Shawn winked and smiled at her in a provocative sexual way.

"Okay then. We'll meet you at Sony,"

Denise yelled back, "I got you, babe."

Everyone got into their respective rides and headed over to Sony to continue to celebrate.

"Sexiful, baby, I never experienced anything like that before. I was blown away when you said that was your daughter and your grandson walking down the runway. But, baby, you look so young to have a daughter that finished med school and a grandson in college. He's acting and modeling part-time. Baby, you are so lucky. I just pray that my son grows up to go to college and become someone special."

"He will. Just give him a chance. He is already special. Things will work out. Shawn, I worked for what I have. None of this was given to me. Baby, I worked real hard to have all of this. To have what I have, it takes hard work and dedication. It is not an overnight thing, hard work, baby." He nodded.

They all arrived at Sony at the same time. La'Roc looked over to Ms. Holiday. "Ms. Holiday, are you all right?"

"Yes, I'm fine. I need to kiss your daughter and your grandson. They looked so beautiful walking down the runway together."

"Thank you, Ms. Holiday. They just walked into the restaurant talking about their new rides. You'll find them inside."

"Okay, I'll go inside and talk to them." Ms. Holiday turned and walked away toward the restaurant, smiling.

As they entered the restaurant, Chantal and Denise were waiting to start with the questions about Shawn. Shawn seemed to be getting a little nervous around her family and friends. "Hey, handsome, just hang in there, you'll be okay. It's going to be all right, trust me, sweetheart. They love you already."

He smiled and put his hands around her waist.

They all ordered their meals and drinks and enjoyed the rest of the evening, laughing and talking with each other.

As the evening came to a close, Shawn made a toast to the family and thanked everyone for including him in their beautiful night. The ride uptown was great. La'Roc's mother decided to stay with her in Manhattan and leave early the next morning. La'Roc decided to invite everybody to stay the night with her in Manhattan. They all agreed to stay overnight.

Once they arrived at the condo, all the girls ran upstairs to change.

"Why not make a real night of it?" Denise suggested.

"Let's call over Martin and Jerry too."

Chantal agreed. Chantal said, "What the hell, why not?"

La'Roc shrugged. Chantal and Denise took out their cell phones and called their boyfriends to come and stay over. Jerry and Martin agreed and said they would be over within a half hour. All three women went upstairs to set up one of the guestrooms where they would be staying. Just as they had finished fixing up the room, Jerry and Martin arrived. They entered, and their girlfriends took their bags and showed them where they would be staying. After everyone was settled in, they decided to have drinks in the playroom. Everyone raised their glasses and gave La'Roc's daughter and grandson a huge congratulation on the beautiful job they had done on the runway. It was the greatest show on earth. That's how La'Roc felt.

After a couple drinks, everyone was ready for bed. They all went to their assigned rooms. Shawn followed her upstairs to the master bedroom.

Shawn and La'Roc slept, wrapped in each other's arms. It wasn't long before she drifted off to sleep. The next morning, Ms. Holiday called over the intercom and inquired about breakfast. La'Roc looked over at the other side of her bed; it was empty. She could hear the shower running in her bathroom. Shawn was already up and in the shower.

"Ms. Holiday, whatever you cook will be fine. Thank you."

After he came out of the shower, Shawn held her tight and kissed her. "I love you, Sexiful. Please let me take you to that place that I promised you on our first date. Remember, I told you I wanted to take you to a place that you have never been. You remember that? Trust me to love you like I want to. That is all I ask of you for now. Baby, I have to leave for work. I will talk to you soon."

"I love you too, Shawn." She kissed him gently, and then Shawn left for work. She watched him walk down the walkway. La'Roc was happy that he didn't look back because her eyes were tearing. She went into the bathroom to wash her face and brush her teeth. After that, she went to the kitchen to join everyone else that were already at the table, eating the wonderful breakfast that Ms. Holiday had prepared.

Everyone complimented Ms. Holiday on her cooking. Afterward, everyone but La'Roc's mother left and headed on their way home.

"I like that guy," Geneva said once they were alone. "Shawn is a nice fellow. He has very good manners. His mother must have raised him right. Shawn is tall and handsome the way you like your man. He's just the kind of guy I wanted you to end up with." They laughed and slapped her hand as she was giving her a high five.

"Well, Mom, you taught me to pick the good-looking ones only." They laughed again.

"He's way better than that last one you had. What was his name again? Roger." Geneva shook her head.

Speaking of Roger, La'Roc remembered that she had promised to help with his case. She also remembered the new case she had picked up—the Sanchez case. "Yeah, Mom. He's way better. I have to prepare for a few upcoming cases I have."

"Get to work!" her mother said.

She walked into her workroom and started to go over Ms. Sanchez's story about her husband's case. She placed a call to her partner, Mr. Power. She got his voice mail and left a message for him to call her back. After making a few phone calls and writing a few notes, she decided to go for a long walk around the grounds with Paris and Biscuit. They ran all over the place; they were so excited to play with their mommy. La'Roc fell on the lawn, laughing her ass off.

She noticed Ms. Holiday waving her hand for her to come back to the condo. When she got to the door, Ms. Holiday handed her the phone.

"There's a lawyer on the phone."

"Thank you, Ms. Holiday," she said as she took the phone and walked back to her workroom.

"Hi, Mr. Lawyer, what's on your mind?"

"I got your message about the Sanchez case. Let's work together. It will be like old times, ha, ha, ha," Mr. Power said.

"That's funny to you, hon? Okay, we'll get an early start going upstate to see Mr. Sanchez. After reading the information that I e-mailed you, what did you think?"

"Well, La'Roc, there is a lot of holes in the witness's story. I think we might just have a case."

"Okay, if you say so. You are the next best lawyer in the state because I'm number one," she said jokingly.

"Dream on, baby," Alex laughed and hung up the phone.

La'Roc went into the bathroom and turned on the shower. Today was going to be a day of relaxation. After her shower, she decided to join her mother, who was sitting in the den. Ms. Holiday took Paris and Biscuit outside so they could release more of their pent-up energy.

She and her mother talked for a while before La'Roc decided to take a nap. Her nap was full of dreams about Shawn. Just as her dreams were getting ready to get good, the phone woke her up. It was her dream boy, Shawn.

"Hi, Sexiful, what time are we on for tonight?"

"I'll be ready around seven thirty or eight. Is that good?"

"Yeah, that's cool. I have a surprise for you tonight. Don't bother to ask because I'm not telling you."

"Fine, I am all right with that," she said.

"Sexiful, I miss you. I got to go back to work."

"See you tonight." La'Roc smiled as she pressed the End button on her phone. "I wonder what it could be," she said out loud.

She got up and kissed her mother on the forehead while she was still sleeping. She went into the gym to do her afternoon exercise. She thought about the beautiful time she had with her family the night before. After the workout, she grabbed her phone and placed some calls to Chantal and Denise and her sister. She called her daughter to ask her to come over before she left for California. "Sorry, Mom, I wish I could come over. I'm trying to pack the rest of my things. I'm leaving for California tomorrow."

"its okay, Courtney. Next time, I just have to take a trip to Cali and visit you."

"That would be nice," Courtney said.

"Where's my grandson?"

"He should be at his hotel. Don't you remember? He leaves to go back to Washington tomorrow."

"That's right. Let me call him and wish him a safe trip. Love you, Courtney."

"Love you too, Mom."

La'Roc disconnected their call and quickly dialed her grandson. He didn't answer, so she left him a message telling him she loved him. She wished him a safe trip back to school and told him to enjoy his new SUV but to be careful. They hadn't even left yet, but she missed them already.

"Ms. Holiday, will you please toss a green salad, seafood platter, and chill a bottle of white wine for my guest tonight? You can set up everything in the large dining room. Thank you."

La'Roc went to her bedroom and searched her closet. She decided to wear her pink Juicy Couture sweat suit. Her sister, L'Oreal, arrived shortly after. They spent their time telling jokes about Aunt Jenny and Uncle Bob, the drunks of the family, while they waited for Chantal and Denise to arrive for their lunch date.

"I remember one time during Thanksgiving, Uncle Bob set Aunt Jenny's hair on fire. They were both as drunk as a skunk. She didn't even realize her hair was on fire until Uncle Bob started smacking her in the head with an oven mitt. I laughed so hard until I cried," La'Roc said; she was laughing so hard her sides hurt.

"Wow! You still remember that?" her sister asked, laughing hard.

"Why wouldn't I? I'm older than you, remember?"

The two sisters chitchatted about the good memories they had for a while before Chantal and Denise came in.

"Ms. Holiday, we'll be back. We're going to take a walk to pass the time and wait for Denise and Chantal to arrive." Chantal and Denise arrived as soon as La'Roc walked out of the door for their walk. "Take care of Paris and Biscuit."

"Okay, Ms. La'Roc. Enjoy yourself."

The four ladies piled into her Lexus SUV and headed to Al's Seafood Diner. While they waited for their food, the women hounded La'Roc with questions about Shawn. She was more than happy to talk about him. Two hours later, the group was ready to head out.

"I have to get ready for tonight. Shawn called earlier and said that he has a surprise for me. I can't wait to find out what is it," La'Roc said, blushing. Once they got back to La'Roc's condo, the women split up. Her sister got in her car, and Chantal piled into Denise's car.

"We'll talk tomorrow, ladies," La'Roc said as she waved good-bye to them and headed inside.

"La'Roc, I'll drop Mom off. I am going to her house anyway to pick up something."

"Yes, that will be fine sis."

"Ms. Rose, there is a message from a Mr. Powers. He said it's urgent," her housekeeper informed her once she entered the house.

"Thanks." She walked over to the answering machine and hit the Play button. After listening to the message, she took out her cell phone and called Alex.

"Hey, Alex, it's La'Roc," she stated after he answered.

"Let's take that ride today to see Mr. Sanchez. He is being arraigned today and doesn't have adequate representation."

"Sure, that sounds good to me. Meet me at my office in an hour," La'Roc said.

"Please, I hope you don't drive like an asshole. You know you and your reckless driving," Alex joked.

"See you soon," she said, and then hung up.

"I'll call you, Ms. Holiday. I am going to meet my partner to discuss a few cases." Ms. Holiday nodded.

La'Roc jumped in her BMW and went on her way to her office. Alex was already there. He got in her car, and they headed for Upstate Correctional Facility to see Mr. Sanchez.

"I called his wife and informed her of our plans to see him today. She was pleased that we were working on her husband's case," Alex said. They talked about how they were going to present the case the whole entire ride to the Upstate Correctional Facility.

Once Mr. Sanchez was brought into the room and unchained, Alex and La'Roc introduced themselves; Mr. Sanchez greeted them and shook their hands.

La'Roc felt the strength in his handshake, and she could feel he was a hardworking man. His eye contact showed honesty and, of course, fear.

Mr. Sanchez was a handsome tall man.

His expression in his face showed uncertainty.

"Mr. Sanchez, would you please be seated and give us a full description of what happened on the night in question."

Mr. Sanchez explained to Alex what happened that night and what the circumstances around them were. He was being charged with murder in the shooting death of a twenty-one-year-old gang leader who hated cops.

"The boy pulled out his gun first. I pulled out my weapon, announced that I was a cop, and told him to drop his gun. He started firing and shot me in the leg. I had no choice but to fire back. There is a witness that can cohobate my story. We were in a night club. There were plenty of witnesses."

"Mr. Sanchez, who was your lawyer working on the case before your wife contacted me?" La'Roc asked.

His name was Mr. Huffman; he answered, "Mr. Huffman said he never liked me ever since the first day I joined the force. He called me names and talked about my family all the time. He told me that he was going to let me rot in jail. Mr. Huffman said I should go back to my country and die. Please get me out of here, Ms. Rose. I trust you to do the right thing."

"You're being arraigned in about an hour. We'll get you out of this place today. We'll set up a conferences with the victim's attorney. As long as you're being completely honest with me and my partner, Mr. Sanchez, you have nothing to worry about," La'Roc said confidently. They continued to discuss the details of the case until it was time for court.

After the usual introduction proceedings and the swearing in of all respectful parties, Judge Doback asked for the people's request for bail.

"We ask that the defendant be held without bail, Your Honor," the DA said.

"Your Honor, that's outrageous." La'Roc stated Ms. Sanchez be released on his own reconnaissance. "My client is a decorated officer of the law for many years. He isn't a flight risk. We ask that Mr. Sanchez be released on his own reconnaissance."

The judge looked at Mr. Sanchez for a moment and agreed with La'Roc. "Mr. Sanchez, you are hereby released. You are to show up in a week for proceedings."

With that, he slammed down his gavel and walked through the doors behind his stand. At that moment, Mr. Sanchez started to cry and praying in Spanish. "Are you ready to go home, Mr. Sanchez?" Alex asked. He nodded his head in agreement.

"You are the best," he said to La'Roc as he gave her a big embrace.

"Just remember we are not out of the woods yet. It looks like this case is going to trial. Tonight you can go home to be with your family and meet me at my office tomorrow morning. Mr. Sanchez, we are on the same page, right?"

Mr. Sanchez, who still had tears in his eyes, nodded. He was speechless. "Come on," Alex said, "we'll take you home now."

The trio exited the courthouse and piled into La'Roc's car. She gave Mr. Sanchez her cell phone so he could call his wife and give her the good news. The drive home was long and boring. Alex and Mr. Sanchez fell asleep before they were even halfway home.

La'Roc decided to pop in a CD to keep herself awake. She pressed her foot on the gas pedal and did eighty all the way home.

They dropped Mr. Sanchez off at home. He and his wife expressed their gratitude once again. La'Roc drove Alex to her office to retrieve his car. "Thanks, Alex, for helping me with the Sanchez's case. I don't understand that man staying in prison as long as he did for defending himself. I got news for that Mr. Huffman. If I find out that he has been tampering with evidence, I will have his license by the end of the week. You feel me, Alex?"

"Yes, I feel you, Ms. Lawyer. Huffman has no idea who he's up against."

"Check out Mr. Huffman's background. I need it like yesterday."

"Okay. I am on it," Alex said. "See you tomorrow, thanks, babe."

She decided to give Shawn a call. "Hello, baby, I missed you today," she said once he answered.

"Hi, Sexiful, I missed hearing from you today and seeing your lovely face. I can't wait until tonight. Please say that you missed me so much that you can't live another minute without me. Please, Sexiful, say you missed me."

"Yes, Shawn, I missed you. Meet me in Westchester as fast as you can. I want to see you now!" They both laughed. People in their cars were looking and laughing at her as she laughed loudly in her car.

"Sexiful, I will see you tonight. Love you."

It was 5:30 p.m. when she arrived at her town house. She missed Ms. Holiday and her two babies, who were still at her condo in Manhattan. But she needed some alone time with Shawn. To help pass the time until Shawn picked her up, she decided to take a long run in the park near her home. She ran three miles. When she returned home, she decided to do a couple sets of her Pilate's routine before jumping into her whirlpool to relax. After another forty-five minutes, she made herself a dry martini and got into her whirlpool for a relaxing soak.

Sitting in her whirlpool, her mind drifted to thoughts of Shawn. She thought back to when they first met and how persistent he was. She laughed to herself when she thought of how hard she tried to play Shawn. His smile was to die for, and he was so funny. He made her laugh without even trying.

He always looked good in whatever he wore, including his work uniform. He was very particular about the way he dressed. Shawn always smelled like he just stepped out of a shower. As she continued to think about Shawn, she began to drift off to sleep.

She was dreaming about Shawn and his son's mother. Denise's phone call woke her up.

"Hi, girl, what's happening?" Denise asked.

"Oh, I am relaxing in the whirlpool. I was just falling asleep. Good thing you woke me up. I was dreaming about Shawn's ex-girl."

"Why? What's that bitch's name anyway?"

"Her name is Kelly Brown," La'Roc answered. "From what I hear, she is a piece of work. She's a fool to pass up a good man like Shawn. I'm glad she did though. I know he loves me, and that is no lie. The ways Shawn made love to me, the way he held me close to his chest. I'm going to love him as long as I can. Maybe one day, he will leave me. Lord knows, I really hope not. If Shawn leaves me, I will never love again, especially not the way I love Shawn."

The two friends chatted a little while longer before La'Roc cut the conversation short to get ready for her date with her handsome prince.

"Okay, sis, let me know if you want me to kick some ass like Ms. Kelly Brown. You know I'll fucking do it, La'Roc."

"Yes, I know that you will. Let's not do it tonight, okay?"

"You know I got your back," Denise said with a serious tone. "Chantal will be back from her vacation on Saturday, so keep that day open. I have plans for you two."

"Okay, see you soon."

"Love you."

"I love you too." She ended the call and laid the phone down on the side of the pool.

Chantal was out of town. She went to Japan on a doctor's conference. La'Roc smiled to herself as she thought about her friends. She had known Denise and Chantal ever since her college days. They had always been there for her no matter what, and she was there for them. They were just like sisters. She loved them both a great deal. They were a part of the reason she was certain that Shawn was the right one for her. They liked him, and their opinions held a lot of weight. They never tried to hide their disdain for Roger. They would always tell her, "Get away from that no-good man before he takes you down with him because he will go down one day, and I want you to get as far away from him as possible. He is very jealous of you and what you have become." They couldn't have been any more correct.

Roger would always be Roger—petty and stupid. He would be a good lawyer if he would stop trying to fuck every woman in the courthouse and focus on his cases. He needed to focus more on his clients and stop trying to be Mr. Big Shot.

She finished her martini and jumped out of the whirlpool. She dried off and went into the master bedroom to get dressed for her date with Shawn. She couldn't wait to see the surprise he had for her.

While contemplating what to wear, she decided to give Ms. Holiday a call to make sure she was okay and to check on her babies.

"Yes, Ms. Rose, we are all fine and enjoying ourselves. Don't worry about us. Enjoy yourself tonight. We will see you soon."

"Thank you so much, Ms. Holiday, for everything." They ended their call. La'Roc thought about Ms. Holiday and smiled. She was really thankful for her. She knew that her housekeeper genuinely loved her and her puppies. She felt the same way about her. "She's great," La'Roc said aloud.

La'Roc decided to dress extra sexy that night. She walked into her walk-in closet and pulled down a purple Donna Karan dress with a low V-cut that ran down to her navel with a slit in the back. She knew that Shawn would like that Donna Karan dress on her sexy body.

She moisturized her entire body and fell across the bed since she still had some time to kill before Shawn arrived. She let one of her favorite CDs play while she relaxed. Her cell phone began to ring. Hoping it was Shawn calling to say that he was going to be early, she jumped up. "Hello," she answered eagerly.

"Hi, Sexiful, I'm going to be about thirty minutes late. I'm sorry, babe. I will be there as soon as I can, okay, Sexiful?"

She frowned. "Shawn, whatever you have to do, just hurry. I will be here waiting for you with a nice drink. Okay?"

"Sounds good, baby, and don't forget to stir it with your finger. I want to taste you in my drink." He laughed.

"I got you, babe," La'Roc answered with a smirk.

She rolled off her king-size bed to the floor and went into the kitchen to get an apple. Afterward, she went into the lounge to put a bottle of champagne on ice and waited for her young stud to arrive.

Still listening to her music, she fell asleep in the living room. Again, she was dreaming about Shawn's ex-girlfriend.

The phone ringing woke her up.

"Hi, Sexiful, I'm outside. You want to buzz me in?"

La'Roc got up quickly and buzzed her lover in. She unlocked the front door.

"Hey, babe, missed me?" Shawn asked when he walked in.

"You know I did. What do you want first, me or your drink?" she asked, playing around.

"I want both. However, I will take the kiss first. Come to daddy, Sexiful, and act as though you've missed me." She ran into his arms. "I love you, Sexiful, please don't ever leave me. I don't think I could live without you."

"I love you too, Shawn. Let's not talk about that right now. Just hold me in your arms and love me like I am the only woman in the world."

After a short embrace, she led him to the room and poured out two glasses of the chilled champagne.

"Baby, we need to talk. Lately, I've been having these bad dreams about Kelly. What's going on, Shawn? Is there something I need to know?"

"Sexiful, I told you Kelly and I have nothing going on. We share a son together, and that is all. We are finished, and I mean that from the bottom of my heart. I love only you."

"Shawn, I just can't help but to feel that something bad is going to happen because we are too happy." La'Roc sat down next to him.

"Baby, let me love you. Trust me, I will show you that I am yours and yours only."

"Shawn, I trust you more than you will ever know. If you only knew how much I love being with you, waiting on your phone calls.

You make me feel like a young teenager waiting for her date to take her to the prom."

"Sexiful, let's stay in tonight."

"Okay. That's all right with me."

Shawn pulled her into his arms and kissed her real aggressively. She loved every minute of his passion. She ran her fingers through Shawn's hair and reached down to awaken his manhood. She popped the button from his Versace shirt to expose his sexy six-pack. Kissing his chest, she could smell his Calvin Klein cologne. The scent of him turned her on even more.

Hungry for his love, she began to flick his left nipple with her tongue. The sensation excited Shawn so much that he let out a loud moan. The sound of his moans turned La'Roc on like she had never been turned on before. She possessed a special trait that turned him on every time. Shawn called it knowing how to satisfy your man. Denise would call it being a freak. She continued to lick his chest and caress his penis. Shawn began to make loud and strange noises. She placed her fingers over his lips. Within moments, he took her fingers and placed them into his mouth. She felt as if she was about to explode. As his hands slowly moved across her body, he slipped two fingers into her womanhood. He knew what she wanted, and he gave her his all. He knew what to do to make her call him names that neither of them had ever dreamed off.

Shawn picked her up and carried her into the bedroom to continue to make love to her body and soul. He had a way of making love to her that made her feel like she was on another planet.

They made love for what seemed to be hours, but it was all good. After they finished, they took a shower together and had a glass of wine. They finally went to bed in each other's arms. He liked it when she laid her head on his chest. She could sleep in that position all night. He held her close to his warm body, and she felt good lying in his strong arms; she never wanted him to leave. At that moment, she was sure that he was her man and she was his lover forever.

He kissed her on the forehead and whispered, "Sexiful, just for the record, I do love you." She drifted off to sleep.

The next morning, Shawn woke her up. "Come on, sleepyhead, it's time to go for your morning jog in the park. Let's go."

La'Roc didn't budge.

"I'm going to count to ten. If you're not up, I'm going to drag you into the shower." He began to count to ten. La'Roc started laughing, but still didn't move. He finished counting and attempted to pull her out of bed, but she rolled to the opposite side, trying to escape his grasp and fell on the floor. "Baby, are you all right?" There was no answer. He walked over to the other side of the bed where she laid on the floor. When he bent down beside her to see if she was okay, she leapt up and slapped him with a pillow. "Are you kidding me? I'm here scared as hell. I thought something happened to you when you fell off the bed."

"Oh, Shawn, please don't be angry. It was all in fun."

"Baby, I love you too much to let anything happen to you. If something happens to you, I don't know what I will do."

She could see the concern on his face and the sincerity in his voice. "I'm sorry," she said as she kissed him.

They got up off the floor, got themselves together, and went for a morning jog. She thought about her babies, Paris and Biscuit. She missed them. Ms. Holiday would be bringing them home tonight. She couldn't wait to see her running partners.

After they finished running three miles, they headed back to the house to do some Pilates. They decided to do workout an extra hour and a half. After about twenty minutes into Pilates, Shawn was exhausted. He excused himself, and La'Roc continued her workout. The smell of breakfast filled the air. She stopped her workout and headed toward the kitchen.

"Sit down, babe, and let me serve you your breakfast," Shawn said with a smile that stretched from ear to ear. He laid out a feast of blueberry pancakes, egg whites, turkey bacon, and orange juice.

"Thanks, Shawn, it smells really nice and looks delicious."

Shawn served her food, and they sat down together and had breakfast.

"That was excellent, Shawn. Thanks for breakfast, sweetheart. Dinner is on me tonight."

"Thanks for last night, it was wonderful," Shawn laughed as he kissed her cheek. He asked her about her plans for the day.

"I have to see the judge this morning about the case I'm working on. You remember the Sanchez case?"

"Oh right, well, good luck with that, babe. I have to go to work now."

After Shawn left, La'Roc got dressed and drove off to work. It was a beautiful day. The wind was blowing in her hair just the way she liked it. She was heading south on I-95. She looked at herself in her rearview mirror. She looked good in her white suit, green silk shirt, and three-inch green heels.

Mr. Sanchez and Alex were standing in front of the courthouse, waiting for her.

"Good morning, Mr. Sanchez, Alex. Are you ready to win this case?" La'Roc said as she walked up to them.

"Yes, we are. Well, let's go beat some ass," Alex said cheerfully.

"How do you feel, Mr. Sanchez?"

"I feel great, Ms. Rose. My wife is grateful as well."

"Will she be in court today?"

"Yes, she will be there."

"Mr. Sanchez, there is something that we haven't discussed," La'Roc stated as the trio walked into the courtroom. "During this case, we may want you to testify. Is that a problem?"

"No, Ms. Rose, for me to testify will not be a problem. I just want to tell the court what happened that night. I'm not guilty. I didn't do anything wrong that night."

La'Roc smiled.

They entered the courtroom where the proceedings where to be held. As they passed, La'Roc heard one police officer say, "Wow! Look who he has for his lawyer. Wonder how he managed to get a high-priced lawyer like her to handle his case." The two officers smirked. La'Roc rolled her eyes and kept walking down the aisle. Those that were gathered around the prosecutor's table weren't pleased to see her walking in with Mr. Sanchez. They knew Ms. La'Roc would get to the bottom of the bullshit.

Court was in session. The court officer car ried on with the usual announcement of the case number and the attending parties. He asked everyone to rise as the judge walked in. After he was seated, everyone else was able to sit.

"Mr. Sanchez," the judge started, "this court understands that you are here today charged with the shooting death of a twenty-one-year-old male after a brawl in a night club. Is this correct?"

"Yes, Your Honor, that is correct."

"You've entered your plea of not guilty. And you have counsel here to represent you in this case." Mr. Sanchez nodded and looked over to La'Roc and Alex. "Are the people ready to start proceedings today?"

The DA stood up. "Yes, we are, Your Honor. We are more than ready." The DA presented his opening statement. The picture that he portrayed of Mr. Sanchez was that he was a drunken cop out for revenge against gang members. After spotting them in the night club, he started a brawl and opened fire, shooting the victim, Ralph Fields, and an innocent man who also happened to be the gang leader's brother.

La'Roc smiled to herself. That was just what she thought he would do—portray her client to be some type of villain. She looked over her notes one last time and waited for the DA to finish his charade. When he was done, he took his seat. La'Roc stood up and cleared her throat. She faced the jury box. "Ladies and gentleman, Mr. Sanchez has been a dedicated police officer for the last twenty years. He has dedicated his life to cleaning up the streets of New York. He is a highly decorated officer of the law who, in fact, had just been promoted to detective the night of this incident. He and a few fellow officers were out celebrating his promotion. Throughout the duration of this trial, you will hear testimony from other police officers who can testify on the behalf of Mr. Sanchez and tell you how the victim, his brother, and several other gang members instigated this horrific accident. You will hear testimony from doctors who will explain the trajectory and angles of the bullet wounds that both Mr. Sanchez as well as the victim, Mr. Fields, suffered. They will help you understand how my client was firing his weapon in self-defense. The district attorney will try and persuade you to believe that Mr. Sanchez was a vengeful cop looking to take out this gang. By the end of this trial, you will come to one conclusion and one conclusion only. That is that this accident was nothing more than that—an accident. You have no other option but to find him not guilty. I look forward to your verdict at the end of this trial. Thank you for your time, ladies and gentlemen." La'Roc, satisfied with her opening statement, took a seat next to Alex. The judge called for a continuance. The parties gathered their thing and headed out the courthouse.

La'Roc and Alex talked briefly about when they would meet up again to discuss the next leg of their case. Mr. Sanchez and his wife got into their car and headed home. La'Roc got into hers and headed north to her town house.

As she drove along Highway 95, her cell started to ring.

Her first thought was that it was Shawn calling. She looked at the screen; it was her daughter calling from California. "Hi, baby, what's up?" she answered.

"I just called to say I love you and I miss you, Mom."

"Baby, I miss you too. As a matter of fact, I was thinking about visiting you this week. Is that all right?"

"Oh, Mom, that would be great. Your grandson's supposed to be coming for a visit this weekend too. It will be great to have you two here together."

"Sweetheart, is everything all right? You just don't sound like your old self. Talk to your old mom, kid."

"Oh, Mother. I'm all right. Are you bringing Shawn with you?"

"No, I was thinking of asking your grandmother and your aunt to take the trip with me. You know your old-fashioned aunt though she would probably want to walk to California."

"Or take a bus," Courtney added. They both laughed. They chatted for a little while longer before they hung up.

The rest of her ride home was on Courtney. After that call, she was a little worried about her. Once she got settled inside, she called Shawn and shared her feelings with him about her daughter.

"Sexiful, it will be all right."

"I know, baby."

"Hey, babe, I can be there in an hour."

"No, Shawn, I'm okay. I will see you tomorrow. We will have the whole day to play."

"Okay, Sexiful, see you tomorrow. If you need me, please remember I'm only a phone call away." They hung up the phone.

Ms. Holiday was on her way to the town house with Paris and Biscuit. She couldn't wait to see them. The tone of her daughter's voice during their phone call still disturbed her. Thinking to herself, she thought maybe she should leave tonight. She called the airport to check for flights out tonight. She knew Shawn would be a little angry, but he would get over it. She had to check on her daughter. After making her reservations, she placed a call to a friend of hers in California that she went to law school with. His name was Jordan Diaz He was a damn good lawyer. He was as good as she was. Jordan had a crush on her when they were in law school. She opted to be his friend. To this day, they remained good buddies. After they spoke briefly, she said, "I need you to go over to my daughter's condo and check on her. I'm a little worried about her and this new guy."

"Don't worry about it, I'm on it. I will call you as soon as I arrive at her place," he said. She thanked him and then hung up.

She began to pack when, moments later, she heard Ms. Holiday, Paris, and Biscuit enter.

"Hi, babies! Did you miss Mommy? I missed you." They played for a little while as Ms. Holiday watched from the doorway. "Did they behave themselves?" La'Roc asked.

"Of course they did. They were little sweethearts. I'm going to give them their baths. I see you're packing. Going on a trip?" Ms. Holiday inquired.

La'Roc told her about her concerns about Courtney.

"Ms. La'Roc, don't worry about your daughter. She will be all right. Let me pack your bags for you. You just relax."

"Thank you so much. I know she'll be all right. I just need to go see her." Her ringing cell phone interrupted their conversation. It was Shawn. "Baby, are you home? I need to talk to you about something important."

"Yes, I'm in Westchester."

"Okay. I'll be there shortly."

Moments later, Shawn called from the front gate to let her know he had arrived. She went and opened the door.

Shawn walked in with his head down and a depressed look on his face; he was far from his normal happy self.

"Baby, what's wrong?"

"Sexiful, I love you very much. Please don't leave me. I need you in my life." He grabbed her and held her as tight as he could.

"Shawn. What's going on? Let me go, you are hurting me."

"Baby, I'm sorry. I will never hurt you. Sexiful, I need to tell you something, and what I am about to tell you, you must believe me."

Feeling a bit uneasy, La'Roc said, "Please say what you have to say, Shawn."

He sighed; it seemed like it was the longest sigh she had ever heard. "My son's mother is going around telling people that she is pregnant with my child. Baby, you need to know that's a lie. I have not been with her since I met you. Baby, I'm so happy with you. I don't need her. You're all I need. I love you so much, I can't let you go, and I won't let you go."

She pushed Shawn back a few steps. "Shawn, I can't deal with this baby-momma-drama shit. I have my own child that I need to worry about. I told you about that girl. You can leave my house now and tell me about it later. I'm packing."

"Sexiful, please tell me where you are going."

"I'm going to visit my daughter. Like I said, I have my own child to worry about."

"Sexiful, please don't leave angry with me. I swear, this child is not mine, and I will prove it as soon as you return from your trip."

"Shawn, right now all I would like for you to do is leave."

"Okay. I have to respect that. But, baby, remember I love you and no one else. Sexiful, I would like to take the trip with you. I want to be wherever you are."

"You got some shit to take care of. Fix it, Shawn, or forget that I ever existed in your life."

"Sexiful, I love you more than life. Always believe that. I'll see you when you return, and everything will be like it was before this lie started. Sexiful, if I didn't love you, I wouldn't have told you about all this bullshit. I would have taken care of it without you even knowing. Think about it! Loving you made me tell you because I don't ever want to lie to you."

La'Roc headed over to the door and opened it, hoping Shawn would take the strong hint she was giving him. As Shawn walked out the door, she started to cry because she loved him too and never wanted to let him go. She really felt that they were soul mates and would always be together.

They're soul mates and will always be together. She wanted to take him into her arms and tell him that it would be okay. She just couldn't deal with his problems right now. She had to make sure her child was okay. She decided she would deal with Shawn and really hear him out when she got back from California.

She dressed in a pair of sweatpants and a matching top.

She pinned her hair up and called Ms. Holiday downstairs to give her instructions on what to do while she was away.

She left for the airport in her green BMW, speeding. Her cell phone began ringing; she answered. It was Shawn on the other end.

"Baby, I will see you when I return, okay? Everything is going to be all right, I promise."

"Sexiful, I just wanted for you to hear me and trust me. I will wait. Love you." La'Roc hung up the phone. Her phone began to ring again. She answered it without looking at the screen. "I said we talk when I get back."

It was Ms. Holiday. "I'm sorry, Ms. Holiday. What's wrong? Is everything okay?"

"Yes, Ms. Rose. Mr. Parker called, but I told him you would be out of the state. I hope you don't mind."

"That's okay, Ms. Holiday, see you soon."

She parked her car in long-term parking, grabbed her suitcase, headed into the airport, and joined the check-in line. Her mind was in a thousand places.

"Sexiful." She thought she was hearing things. She turned around; it was Shawn holding a red rose in one hand and in the other hand, he had his bags. She started to smile because she was so happy to see him. She knew at that moment that they could face anything as long as they were together.

He walked over to her and held out his arms, and she fell into his open arms. He gave her the rose, and he placed a kiss on her lips. He asked what was going on with Courtney. She explained her concerns.

Then she remembered that Jordan hadn't called her back. She decided to give him a call. He picked up.

"Hi, La'Roc, I was getting ready to call you. Baby girl is all right. We talked for a while. She's good."

La'Roc felt relieved. "I'm all packed and at the airport ready to get on my flight. I have my boy toy with me, is that all right with you?"

"Hey, that's fine, baby. You know that I don't judge you. You're like my sister, and I love you. So if you love him, I know that I will love him too. But you don't ever have to worry about Courtney. She will be fine, just like her Mom—mean as hell!" he chuckled.

"We will see you soon." She ended the call, and then turned all her attention to Shawn. "Baby, I'm so happy that you're going with me to California. I love you, Shawn. Please don't worry about your son's mother. We will fix it as soon as we return to New York"

"Sexiful, please hold me and never let go."

"Baby, I got you, just keep holding on." They were standing in the airport just holding each other. La'Roc looked up into his eyes as tears rolled down his face.

"Shawn, why are you crying? I told you everything will be okay."

"I just love you so much until it hurts, and I don't want to lose you."

"I'm always going to be here. As long as you're honest with me, I'm here to stay. Right now, I'm just focusing on my daughter."

He smiled.

"Shawn, could it be your child that she is carrying? It's okay if we weren't together. Just don't lie to me. We will count back the months, and if it's your child, we will take care of it in court."

He smiled. "I know you are the best lawyer in the world to me. You're the best."

"I have a feeling that I'm going to have a problem with that lady, and my problems are going to be worse than yours. I'll show her if she fucks with me, I will take her son and give him to you. She doesn't know who she is fucking around with. She better recognize that you got a real woman, and I will fight for my man."

They boarded the plane. La'Roc was content that Shawn was with her. She felt safe and protected with him by her side.

When they were seated, she placed her head on his chest and whispered in his ear, and they both laughed out loud. Other passengers looked and smiled.

Although she was going to check up on her daughter, this was going to be a nice little vacation away from her law firm.

She played with the hair on Shawn's chest until she fell asleep. The sound of the pilot announcing their arrival at LA International Airport woke La'Roc up. She woke up Shawn by kissing his soft lips. "Baby, it is time to get off the plane. We're getting ready to land. Wake up, sleepyhead." They exited the plane and got their luggage.

"Baby, I made reservations at the Hilton. It's about two miles from Courtney's condo. We can stay there tonight and go see her in the morning."

"Sexiful, I will pay for the hotel. I can support you. Please allow me to support you with what I have. I'm not rich like you, but I can take care of you. Please give me a chance to show you how much I need and want you to be in my life forever."

"Shawn, please stop saying forever. Forever is a long time, and we can't predict the future, so let's just love each other at the moment."

As they left the airport holding hands, she felt like Superwoman; nothing could touch her and her young man. She asked herself, "Who cares if he's younger than I am?" She was so content when she was with Shawn.

As they waited for La'Roc's car service outside the airport, La'Roc thought she heard someone call her name.

"I thought I heard someone call your name, babe," Shawn said as he looked around.

"Yeah, I heard that too." As she turned around, she saw a handsome tall man holding her daughter's hand. Courtney was smiling from ear to ear. The man that was with her daughter was Jordan. He stood six feet four inches, almost as tall as Shawn. Courtney looked as good as ever with Jordan's baseball cap on her head turned backward. She was wearing a tight sweater and a pair of shorts to match.

They walked over to where La'Roc and Shawn stood. La'Roc was surprised to see her daughter and longtime friend standing there.

"Hey, baby. What are you doing here?" La'Roc asked Courtney.

"I should be asking you that, Mom. Why didn't you tell me you were coming tonight? Uncle Jordan just told me he wanted me to take a ride with him, and here you are!" Courtney said as she hugged her mother. After letting her mother go, Courtney gave Shawn a hug. "Uncle Jordan, come and meet Shawn."

"Oh man, I'm sorry, with all the excitement, I forgot to introduce myself. My name is Jordan Diaz. I'm one of La'Roc's best friends. We have been friends for years."

"I am pleased to meet you, Jordan. My name is Shawn Parker."

"I heard some good things about you, Shawn. Keep it that way because I love her like she's my sister. Take care of her, okay?"

"Jordan, you will never have to worry about me hurting her. She is my world. I too love her too."

As they walked to the limo that the car service sent, Courtney asked her mother, "Where are you guys going?"

"Baby, we made reservations at the Hilton."

"Okay, Mom."

"I'll see you guys for breakfast in the morning, right?"

"Right, oh, your grandson should be here in a few days as well."

After the men were done putting the suitcases in the trunk, they said their good-byes and went on their separate ways.

As La'Roc positioned herself to get comfortable in Shawn's arms, her cell phone started to ring. She looked down to see who was calling her at this hour. It was Chantal. "Hello, Ms. Lady, what the hell you want?"

"What the hell you mean what I want? I want to know why you are in California. What's going on with Courtney? Is she all right?"

"Yes, your godchild is fine. Where are you? Are you still in Japan?"

"Yes, I am and looking forward to coming home this weekend. Are you having fun yet?" Chantal asked.

"Well, we just landed. Courtney and Jordan were at the airport when we arrived."

"Okay, cool. What is Denise up to?"

"Denise is still in Washington doing what she does best—selling homes to rich people. She will be back in NY tomorrow. But hey, girl, enjoy yourself. I will see you when you return to NY. We'll do lunch."

"Okay. Tell Shawn I said hello, and he better treat you right." They both laughed.

"I'm going to be here for a while. Why don't you and Denise join us for a few days?"

"That would be fun. I'll call her as soon as I hang up from you."

"Bye, Chantal, hope to see you soon."

"You will see me in a couple of days."

They ended their call. La'Roc looked over at Shawn; he was fast asleep. She kissed him on his lips very softly and whispered to him, "Sweet dreams, baby."

They arrived at the Hilton, went inside, and checked in. The room was so beautiful; their window faced the Golden Bridge. Shawn held her so tight she thought he was going to break every bone in her little body, but it felt damn good to be in his arms.

"Shawn, why are you so quiet?" she asked.

"Baby, I was just thinking about the two of us getting married and going away and never going back to New York."

"Oh well, that is just wishful thinking. That will never happen. Shawn, let's not talk about not going back to NY." She turned away from the window. "Remember what I told you before we left? I really don't want to talk about what's going on in New York. If it can be fixed, we will fix it, and if not, we will be going our separate ways."

"Please, baby, let's just enjoy our time together." Shawn kissed her forehead. "I love you."

He pulled her close to him. She could hear his heart pounding as if he had just run a marathon. "Come on, let's have a drink and get in the Jacuzzi," he suggested.

"Yes, I could use a drink," La'Roc said. She needed to take Shawn and the drama that awaited her in New York off her mind. He went to the bar that they had passed in the lobby. When he returned, La'Roc was nowhere to be found. "Hey, babe, where did you go?" he called out.

"I'm in the bathroom. Wait by the Jacuzzi. I have a surprise for you."

As Shawn put the drinks down, La'Roc walked up behind him with a short black gown on. "Hey."

"Sexiful, you look good enough to eat."

She walked closer and playfully pushed him into the Jacuzzi with all his clothing on. He looked at her and pulled her into the Jacuzzi with him. They both began to laugh. He stuck his tongue into her mouth. They made passionate love in the Jacuzzi like they were the only two people in the world. Afterward, they drifted off to sleep in each other's arms.

The next morning, La'Roc's ringing cell phone woke Shawn up. La'Roc didn't budge.

"Baby, your phone is ringing. Want me to answer it?" She nodded. "Hello, this is Shawn, who am I speaking to?" It was Courtney. "Sexiful, wake up, it's Courtney on the phone. She wants to speak to you."

"Tell her I'll call her back in about an hour. Sorry we didn't make it for breakfast."

Shawn relayed the message and hung up the phone. Moments later, La'Roc woke up. She went to the bathroom, washed her face, and brushed her teeth. They ordered breakfast. "Let's go for a run," La'Roc suggested. When they finished eating, they got dressed and ran several blocks. When they returned to their room, they took a long hot shower, got dressed, and headed for Courtney's. La'Roc's grandson was supposed to be arriving later on that afternoon. As they got into the car service, La'Roc picked up her phone and dialed Courtney.

"Hi, baby, Mommy is on her way. What do you need?" she asked once her daughter answered on the other end.

"I need you to hurry and get here. I'm planning a cookout. I need you to come and make the potato salad and tell Shawn he could help Jordan with the grill."

"Okay. We're on our way. See you soon, babe. Did Jordan get there yet?"

"Yes, he was here at seven this morning, messing with me and telling dry jokes. Please hurry, I'm tired of his lame jokes." They both laughed.

As they were driving away from the hotel, La'Roc spotted an SUV that looked just like her grandson's. *Oh well, I could be wrong*, she thought. As they got on the freeway, La'Roc looked out of the window and again thought she saw her grandson's SUV. She didn't say anything to Shawn, but she watched the SUV like a hawk.

When Shawn and La'Roc arrived at Courtney's house, Courtney had a big poster that read, "Welcome to my home, Mom, Devon, and the man that makes my mom so very happy, Shawn Parker." La'Roc began to tear. They walked throughout the house, looking for Courtney. People had already begun to arrive for the cookout. They went to the rear of the house. The pool was surrounded with people dressed in their bathing suits. The music was blaring.

As she scanned the backyard, someone walked up behind her and covered her eyes with their hands. La'Roc turned to see who it was. It was her grandson, Devon. She smiled and gave him a huge hug.

"I thought that you were following us on the freeway."

Devon shook Shawn's hand. "I see you and Grandma are still together. You must be doing something right. I love to see her happy. To see her smile, that's what makes me happy." They shook each other's hand.

"Where's your mother? She wanted me to do something for her, but I can't find her."

"I think she's in the kitchen," Devon said.

La'Roc walked off, leaving Shawn and Devon behind. She found Courtney in the kitchen just as Devon had said. "I'm here. Courtney, are you ready for me to make the potato salad now?"

"Hey, mom." Courtney gave her mother a hug. The two women talked while they cooked. When they were done, La'Roc went to the backyard to look for Shawn. He was standing by the grill, having a good time with Jordan.

"Hey, Shawn, are you ready to eat?"

"Yeah, I sure am," he said as he rubbed his stomach. La'Roc made two plates. They found a spot to eat and listened to music while they ate potato salad, franks with beans, hamburgers, and corn on the cob; everything tasted great.

"Hey, girl, surprise!" La'Roc turned around and saw her two best friends and their boyfriends. She jumped up and gave them both a big hug.

"What are ya'll doing here?"

"We came to surprise you and check up on our goddaughter. You know we don't play when it comes to her," Denise said. Courtney walked over and greeted Chantal and Denise. As La'Roc looked on, she felt like she was the luckiest woman in the world. She was surrounded by her friends, her lover, her daughter, and her grandson. She couldn't have asked for a better day.

"I'm going to go help Jordan on the grill, babe. Have fun," Shawn said, then walked away, leaving the women in a circle, laughing and talking. Devon walked over to Chantal and Denise; they started to tease him about how deep his voice had gotten and how tall he's grown.

"Stop making fun of my boy," Courtney joked. La'Roc loved to see her daughter and grandson interact. It was one of the most beautiful sights she had seen, and it made her feel so happy.

After a few minutes of joking around the grill with Jordan, Shawn walked over to La'Roc. "Hey, babe, are you okay?"

"Yes, I'm okay, what about you?"

"As long as I'm with you, I will always be okay." Shawn kissed her and walked away. As she turned back to face her friends, she noticed Courtney walking back into her house. "Devon, where is your mother going?" she asked.

"Oh, I think she went to talk to Justin."

"Who is Justin?"

"He's her boyfriend, I think," Devon said as he shrugged his shoulders.

La'Roc turned her attention back to her daughter's house just in time to see Courtney and a big guy walking in her direction, hand in hand, smiling.

"Mom, this is Justin. He is a special friend of mine."

La'Roc looked him directly in his eyes and shook his hand firmly. "I am pleased to meet you, Justin."

"Likewise. It's a pleasure meeting Courtney's mother."

At that moment, Shawn walked up. "What's up, babe?"

"Oh, baby, this is Justin. He is a friend of Courtney's."

"Pleased to meet you, man," Justin said as they shook hands. Courtney introduced him to some of the other guests, including Chantal and Denise. Hours later, the cookout was still going on. Everyone was having a good time, enjoying themselves. Courtney made a toast to all her guests, and she thanked them for coming. "Thank you all for welcoming my mother and Shawn to California."

La'Roc decided she wanted to make a toast as well. She walked up beside her daughter. "I would like to make a toast to my daughter and my grandson. You guys are doing a wonderful job, and I am extremely proud of you both." Courtney gave her mom a hug. "I would also like to thank my best friends, my sisters, Chantal and Denise, for flying all the way here just to be with all of us. Jordan was always looking out for my daughter when I can't be here and, last but not least, a toast to my Shawn. Thank you for joining me on this trip."

Jordan left the grill and walked over to La'Roc. He planted a kiss on her cheek. She slyly looked over to Shawn, and she could read the jealousy that was written all over his face.

About an hour later, the cookout started to die down, and everyone began to leave to go home. La'Roc and Shawn said their good-byes to Courtney and Devon and thanked them again for showing them a wonderful time. Chantal and Denise decided to leave then too. They were going to go back to the hotel with La'Roc and Shawn. They chatted for a while as they waited for La'Roc's car service to pick them up. Moments later, they heard a honk coming from the front of the house. It was the car service. La'Roc hugged and kissed her daughter and grandson, and then they piled into the car. Chantal and Denise were following behind them.

La'Roc was so tired she fell asleep before they even turned the corner. "Wake up, baby, we're here," Shawn whispered in her ear as he moved the few strands of hair that had fallen over her face. When she stepped out of the car, she was shocked to see Courtney, Devon, Jordan, Justin, Chantal and Denise, and both of their boyfriends; but most of all, she was surprised to see Ms. Holiday. Jordan and Justin were waiting in front of the hotel.

She looked over to Shawn who had a wide smirk on his face. Ms. Holiday walked up to them and placed a bag at their feet. "Open it," Shawn instructed. La'Roc bent down and slowly peeked inside. La'Roc was surprise when Paris and Biscuit popped out of the bag.

They were *so* happy to see her; they jumped out of the bag and started licking her everywhere.

"Surprise!" everyone yelled. La'Roc couldn't speak. She had missed her babies dearly. She scooped them both up into her arms and kissed them as the group made their way inside to La'Roc's hotel suite.

The party continued once they got upstairs.

"Shawn, when did you have time to do this?"

"I made all the arrangements while you were sleeping this morning."

She leaned over and kissed him gently. "You're the best." She looked around the room and was so pleased. She knew that the people in this room loved and cared for her. There were just two people missing. She reached over to the nightstand and picked up the hotel room phone. She needed to call her mother.

"Devon," she called for her grandson. He got up from the chair he was sitting in by the television. "Would you like to say hello to your great-grandmother? I'm calling her now. Tell your mother to come say hello."

"Okay, Grandma." Devon walked away to go get his mother.

She dialed her mom's number, and after three rings, Geneva answered.

"Hi, Mom, are you busy?"

"Hey, girl, I'm never too busy for you. Where are you?"

"I'm in California with your granddaughter and great-grandson. I told you I was going to make a trip down here. I asked you to come with me, remember?" Courtney and Devon walked in. "Here they are, Mom. Hold on." They talked with Geneva for a few moments before handing the phone back to La'Roc.

"Thanks for calling, baby," Geneva said.

"I'll see you when I get back, Mom. Love you." She ended the phone call and dialed her sister. They chatted for a while. "Courtney, your aunt L'Oreal and Uncle Casey is on the phone. They want to talk to you."

Courtney walked over. "All right, sis, see you when I get back. Love you," she said, and then handed the phone over to Courtney.

Two hours later, the group was ready to call it quits. Courtney, Justin, Jordan, and Devon left. Chantal, Denise, and their boyfriends asked if they could sleep in the living room area as they were too tired and drunk to drive to their hotel. La'Roc agreed. Ms. Holiday headed to the room that Shawn had booked for her. She took Paris and Biscuit with her. "We'll see you in the morning," she said as she exited.

La'Roc and Shawn decided to have a glass of wine and take a dip in the Jacuzzi. They had been waiting all day to fall into each other's arms. As La'Roc looked at her man, she wanted to make love to him right there on the bathroom floor. He picked her up and into his strong arms and carried her into the Jacuzzi. The hot water felt good on their bodies. They made love in the Jacuzzi. La'Roc thought to herself, Shawn felt as good as he licked her all over her body. She cried out, and he gave her everything she asked for and more.

He made love to her like it was their first time. *Oh, I love this man*, she thought. Shawn made love to her like she had never been loved before. She used to go to sleep dreaming about a man making love to her like Shawn was doing right now. She thanked God each and every day for sending Shawn to her. She would never let another woman have him, not in a million years. She said to herself that she will never give up on Shawn,especially to his son's Mother. She couldn't wait to get back to New York to handle Shawn's case against her. She knew that when they returned home, she would have a fight on her hands. She wouldn't let that spoil her moment. She would deal with that in due time. Right now, she just wanted to make love to Shawn all night long. They were breathing like wild animals ready to eat each other up, and she loved every minute of it.

"Love me, Shawn, and don't ever stop loving me," she moaned.

"Sexiful, I will always love you. I'm yours forever, and don't ever forget that."

"Baby, do you really love me? Please say yes and mean it. I will die before I let you go," she said. He stopped and kissed her over and over.

He picked her up and carried her to the bedroom. "Baby, I'm not going anyplace. I'm here to stay, so please don't worry about anything." He laid her gently on the bed. He teased her with his tongue as he kissed her everywhere. He climbed on top of her and stuck his penis deep into her. She begged for more. He gave her all he had. She was moaning and begging for more. He gave her all of what she asked for. That night, they made love like never before. They fell asleep in each other's arms.

Every time Shawn made love to her, it seemed to get better and better, La'Roc thought out loud.

Shawn's ringing cell phone disturbed her peaceful sleep. She looked at the clock that rested on the nightstand. It was six in the morning.

She tapped him on his shoulder. "Baby, wake up, your phone is ringing."

"Answer it please," he said as he rolled over. La'Roc reached over and picked up his phone. She looked at the screen; the number was blocked. "Hello," she said.

"Hello. This is Shawn's baby's mother. Can I talk to him?" It was Kelly Brown. La'Roc could sense a bit of attitude in her voice.

"Shawn is sleeping now. May I take a message?" she said, trying to be as polite as possible.

"No, I need to speak to Shawn about his son."

La'Roc sat up on the side of her bed as she said, "Look, sweetheart, I'm Shawn's lawyer. Whatever you have to say to Shawn, you can say it to me."

"Look, I didn't call to speak with you. I just need to talk to him about his plans for his son and the new baby on the way. Now put him on the phone," Kelly demanded.

"I would advise you not to call him again. He will see you in court. Please be prepared to fight. Of course, you are going to lose. I don't care whose mother you are. The case is mine, and you will lose. You will not get him back, so live with that. We will see you Monday morning in court and be ready for a showdown. Make sure you have a good damn lawyer." She hung up the phone before Kelly could get another word in. She placed the phone back on the nightstand and lay back down to continue her sleep.

It felt like she had just closed her eyes when Shawn woke her up with a kiss on the lips. "Good morning, Sexiful."

She opened her eyes and saw Shawn. "Baby, we have to leave tomorrow. We have a court date the first thing on Monday."

He looked confused. She explained to him the conversation she had with Kelly Brown. "Baby, I'm so glad that you are my lawyer. I love you more and more each and every day. I wish I had never met that woman. I wouldn't be in this mess."

"Sweetheart, don't worry, I got your back." They looked at each other and smiled.

"Oh please, I'm not even worried about the case. I know you have my back."

"I'll be back. I'm going to check on Ms. Holiday and the puppies."

"No need," Shawn said. "She stopped by earlier while you were sleeping. She went to take your babies outside."

La'Roc decided to start packing, and Shawn went to the kitchen to make breakfast. After she was done packing, she took a shower while she waited for breakfast.

She could hear Paris and Biscuit scratching at the bathroom door, trying to get in. "Be patient, boys. Your mommy will be out shortly." She could hear Ms. Holiday talking to them.

La'Roc stepped out of the shower and greeted her anxious puppies. She moisturized her body and dressed. Then all her attention was on them. Chantal and Denise had returned from their walk with their boyfriends and joined La'Roc. Mike and John were in the kitchen, talking to Shawn.

Shawn called for everyone to come for breakfast. Everything was set up beautifully, and the food was very tasty. Shawn whipped up some pancakes, eggs, toast, and turkey bacon. The friends sat and ate.

"Chantal, what time are you guys leaving for NY?" La'Roc asked.

"Our flight leaves at five thirty tonight. I leave for Washington tomorrow afternoon."

"Denise, where are you going from here?"

"I'm going back in New York for three days, and then I go back to North Carolina for the closing of this 5million dollar home."

"Damn, we won't see each other for a while. I go to court on Monday to fight with Shawn's son's mother. I need ya'll there to cheer me on."

"Oh, bitch, you know you going to win," Denise said.

Shawn looked at her and winked.

"I still need you there," La'Roc said, smiling.

"Okay, we will be there for your ass then. We will just get a later flight. We all leave tomorrow night then," Chantal said.

"Yeah, that's cool. We will all leave together," Denise added.

After breakfast, Chantal, Denise, and their boyfriends went to the living room. Shawn and La'Roc got dressed and left for Courtney's once the car service picked them up. Ms. Holiday, Paris, and Biscuit went shopping.

As they approached Courtney's house, La'Roc noticed that Devon's SUV was parked in the driveway. She was overjoyed that Devon was spending some time with his mother. She called Courtney from her cell and asked her to open the front door. Shawn got out of the car and walked around to the passenger side to open the car door for La'Roc to get out. Courtney yells from the front door, "What a gentleman you are."

Shawn smiled as he and La'Roc made their way to Courtney.

"Hi, baby, we just stopped by to let you know that we're leaving tomorrow night. I need to see Jordan before I leave. Please call him and ask him to come over. Where's Devon?"

"He's upstairs sleeping. He was up late last night."

"Well, I'm going to wake his butt up. I need to see him before we go back to New York."

Courtney laughed to herself as she made that phone call to Jordan for her mother. When she was done, she yelled from the bottom of the steps to her mother that he would be there shortly.

After messing with Devon for a while, La'Roc joined her daughter in the downstairs living room.

"Courtney, what type of work does Justin do?"

"He works in his father's clothing stores. He is the manager of three stores."

"Did he go to college?" La'Roc pressed on.

"He graduated from the best business school in California, Mom."

"Sweetheart, your happiness is my happiness. I love you, baby. I'm so proud of you. If only your grandfather and Father were here to see your accomplishment, they would be as proud of you as I am." Courtney smiled and walked away with tears in her eyes. She loved her grandfather very much.

Shortly after Jordan arrived, they all chatted for a while; then Shawn and La'Roc said their good-byes. Before they left, Devon handed her a small box and asked her not to open it until she was back in New York. Courtney came up behind him and gave her mother an even bigger box; she made the same request for her mother not to open the box until she arrived back home. La'Roc promised and put both boxes into her Marc Jacobs purse. By the time they got back to the hotel, they were both exhausted; they fell across the bed and drifted to sleep. La'Roc began dreaming about Shawn's court case. She woke up screaming out Shawn's name.

"Baby, please wake up. Wake up." Shawn shook, her, trying to wake her. "What's wrong?" he asked with a look of sincere concern on his face.

"I don't know. I was having some sort of dream about your court case. Shawn, babe, I have a bad feeling about all this."

"Don't worry," he said as he pulled her close. "Everything will be okay. It was just a nightmare. Go back to sleep."

She did feel safe and secure in Shawn's arms.

The next morning, she could feel Shawn getting out of the bed. Moments later, she heard the water running from the shower. She looked over at the time; it was after one o'clock in the afternoon. "Wow. I must have really been tired," she said out loud to herself. She decided to get up and join Shawn in the shower. She quietly opened the bathroom door and, much to Shawn's surprise, slid in the shower behind him. After their shower, they joined Ms. Holiday for breakfast, and then headed to the airport to meet Chantal, Denise, Mike, and John. La'Roc had a wonderful time in California, but it was time to head back to New York to handle her business.

The group met up and checked in. Chantal, Denise, Mike, and John went into one of the restaurants that were in the airport. La'Roc and Shawn declined; they were still full from breakfast.

"Shawn, are you nervous about the case?" La'Roc asked once her friends were gone.

"No, I have nothing to hide."

"Have you thought about the possibility of you being the father of her unborn child?"

"No," he said, "and I don't want you to worry about it either. I'm just concentrating on you and me right now."

La'Roc's phone rang; it was Courtney on the other end.

"Hey, Mom, I'm just checking up on you guys. Making sure you made it to the airport on time."

"Yeah, baby, we're here. I was going to call you once we boarded, but you beat me to the punch," La'Roc said and laughed.

"Okay, Mom, call me once you guys land. Hold on, Uncle Jordan wants to say something to you. Love you, Mom."

"Love you too, baby," La'Roc said and then she waited as Jordan got on the line.

"Hey, baby girl. It was nice seeing you. Hope it's not long before we see you again. Don't worry about your daughter. You know I'm always looking out for her."

"Thanks, Jordan. You take care of yourself too."

"Oh, I always do," he joked.

"Take care of my babies," La'Roc repeated.

"I wouldn't have it any other way. Courtney and Devon are in good hands. Trust me." They hung up the phone.

La'Roc felt kind of weird; Shawn's upcoming case was bothering her. It wasn't like her to be nervous or anxious over a case, but this one was getting to her. She couldn't shake that feeling, no matter how hard she tried.

The stewardess announced over the loudspeaker that their flight would be boarding shortly just as La'Roc's friends returned from having lunch. They boarded the plane. La'Roc looked out the window as the plane took off. Part of her wanted to stay in California.

It wasn't long before they landed in New York. The group made their way to baggage claim and retrieved their luggage. La'Roc scanned the crowd to see if a driver was holding a sign with her name on it. It was then that she remembered that she was in such a hurry to leave and check on Courtney that she drove her BMW and it was waiting for her in the long-term parking lot.

La'Roc made her way over to her car; Shawn and her friends followed. As Shawn gathered their luggage and packed them into the trunk, La'Roc and her friends kissed each other and said their goodbyes. They would all meet up at the courthouse the following morning.

La'Roc climbed into the passenger seat. Ms. Holiday and the puppies were sitting in the backseat. Shawn drove the BMW since he had originally taken a cab to the airport.

As they drove on, Shawn took both of her hands and said, "I want you and the little ones to come to my brownstone and stay over tonight. I have a surprise for you and your babies. Please say that you will go to my place tonight."

La'Roc was surprised. Now that he brought it up, he had never invited her to his house, and she had never thought of asking to go.

"Okay, baby, we'll go with you. Please don't have a heart attack." They both smiled at each other; she placed her head on his shoulder.

"Baby, I am so thankful to have you on my side tomorrow in court. The gratitude that I have for you is unexplainable. I will never be able to repay you for what you are doing for me."

"Shawn, don't thank me until we go over the case because if you are lying to me, there will be hell to pay. You will see my bad side, and it's not pretty. I hope you are telling me the truth about you and Ms. Kelly Brown. I am very serious about my clients telling the truth. Shawn, don't you ever lie to me because if you do, you will be sorry. I take my job very serious. When it comes to my job, I put everything aside, including you, Shawn. I have an excellent reputation in the law world, and I won't allow you or no one else to jeopardize my work. Shawn, you understand that right?" she asked.

"Yes, Sexiful. I know that, and I would never do anything to put your reputation at risk. I know how hard you've worked for it."

La'Roc decided to drop off Ms. Holiday, Paris, and Biscuit at her condo. Shawn pulled up to La'Roc's condo. Shawn parked and helped Ms. Holiday with the luggage upstairs. La'Roc kissed and played with Paris and Biscuit until he returned. "Mommy will be back tomorrow. Love you guys."

"Are you ready to go to Brooklyn?" Shawn asked with a smile that spread from ear to ear. What she was ready to do was take a nice hot shower and go to bed; instead, she said, "Yes, babe. I'm ready."

Ms. Holiday said good night and made her way back to the condo. La'Roc decided to take Paris and Biscuit to Brooklyn with her and Shawn.

La'Roc, Shawn, Paris, and Biscuit were on their way. The whole ride to Brooklyn, Shawn had a smile on his face. She couldn't help but try and guess what kind of surprise he could have waiting for her.

About a half hour later, they pulled up to a beautiful brownstone.

"Well, this is my place," Shawn said as he parked the car.

La'Roc looked out the window. His place was beautiful. He walked around to the passenger side and opened her car door. She got out with her puppies in hand. He led the way into the house. Inside was beautiful and clean. He led her to a back room. To her surprise, he had turned one of his bedrooms into a room for Paris and Biscuit. The room was the same as their room at her condo. Shawn did an excellent job on her babies' room. Paris and Biscuit ran around like they were home.

"Sexiful, come with me, baby. I have something for you too. Close your eyes." He took her hands and led the way. "Open your eyes."

"Oh, Shawn, what have you done? You did all of this for me? Sweetheart, I thank you for my beautiful surprise." He had turned another bedroom into an office and a gym for her and her friends to have a place to hang out in Brooklyn.

Shawn's cell started to ring.

"Answer your cell, baby."

"Hello, this is Shawn. Hold on please, you need to speak to my lawyer. The phone call is for you, Sexiful."

"Who is calling for me on your cell?"

"That is Kelly, my son's mother on the phone."

La'Roc grabbed the phone. "Hello, this is Ms. Rose, Shawn's lawyer, and he has nothing to say to you and please do not call him again. If you call him again, I will get a restraining order on your ass for harassment so fast it will make your head spin. Do you understand me? From this day forward, it will be lawyer to lawyer. I'm hanging up now. Bye, see you in court."

Shawn could sense the tension. "Come on, babe, let's take a shower." They did and then headed for bed. La'Roc was anxious, and tomorrow couldn't come fast enough.

The next morning, La'Roc dressed and got ready faster than she ever had. Chantal and Denise called and said they were on their way to the courthouse. La'Roc and Shawn got into her car.

"I'll drive," Shawn said.

"That's okay, babe, I want to drive."

They got in the car, and La'Roc zoomed off. They reached the courthouse in no time.

Chantal and Denise were outside of the courthouse, waiting for them to arrive. La'Roc instructed them on which part to go to and have a seat. She went and spoke with Kelly's lawyer. He handed her a stack of papers and advised her to go over them quickly.

This woman was all about control. Kelly wanted to use her son to gain control over Shawn's life. She didn't want to share custody of his son; she claimed that he wasn't supportive and did nothing for his son. La'Roc had Shawn's bank statements. He had been sending money to her bank account every month like clockwork. Once they compared the two bank accounts, they would dismiss that claim. Shawn wanted a DNA test since Kelly was supposedly carrying another child for him; La'Roc advised that he did a paternity test on his son too, just to be sure.

La'Roc shook her head in disgust. This woman was trying every trick in the book. Since she couldn't have him, she would try and make his life miserable. For example, dragging him through court proceedings, as if that would make him go back home to her. She was trying to scare him with threatening that he would never see his son again. Same tricks that low-life baby mommas have been trying forever. The case was scheduled for eleven. La'Roc continued to go over the paperwork while she waited for Alex to show.

"Good morning, Ms. Rose. Welcome back." Alex kissed her on her hand as he always did. He sat next to her. "So what do we have here?" he asked.

La'Roc huffed. "It was nothing but a big waste of time. She had no case." She went over the paperwork with Alex as they waited for eleven o'clock.

La'Roc looked behind her to where Shawn and her friends were seated. She noticed him talking to a young woman. She decided to go over to him.

"Hey, babe, we're just about ready to start. Don't worry; this will be over before you know it."

The young woman that Shawn was talking to huffed and stormed away. "Who was that?" La'Roc asked.

"That's my sister, April. Kelly is her best friend, so you can guess what she thinks of this whole court thing. She wants me and Kelly back together. I told her I'm with you now and I'm happy, and I think she should be happy for me. She doesn't get it."

"Well, that's just too bad." She leaned in and kissed Shawn just as Kelly was walking in the courtroom. It wasn't planned, but it was sweet. La'Roc knew that she saw them.

Shortly after, court was in session. Shawn took his place beside La'Roc and Alex. Kelly was a few feet over, sitting next to her lawyer. Her eyes were glued on La'Roc.

The hearing lasted for two and a half hours. The judge ordered joint custody and a DNA test to be done on Shawn's son. The other paternity would be done as soon as the baby was born. Shawn kissed La'Roc on the cheek. She could feel the burning stares of both April and Kelly. They all walked out of the courtroom.

"That woman is a trip. I really don't understand how Shawn put up with her as long as he did. He is a better man than I will ever be," Alex said, and they all began to laugh.

"Alex, take the rest of the day off and come to Brooklyn to Shawn's brownstone so we can celebrate," La'Roc suggested.

Alex said "Taking the day off sounds good. I'm down with that. I will see you in Brooklyn. What time?"

"Around five is good," Shawn said.

"Okay, see you then."

Shawn walked over to Alex and shook his hand. "Thanks, man."

As they were standing in front of the courthouse talking, Kelly and April walked over. "Shawn, you will not get away with this bullshit, I promise you that. You have your high-class lawyer and shit. Just remember, we will be back in court, and I will win."

"Don't entertain the bullshit, babe. Please say bye, Shawn. We'll see you again on the next court date. Good-bye, ladies."

The couple walked off hand in hand, got in La'Roc's car, and drove off. She decided to go to Manhattan and check on Ms. Holiday. As Shawn pulled the car into the garage, La'Roc noticed Ms. Cotton's car parked in the driveway. She was happy that she was back from her trip. "Shawn, Ms. Cotton is back! I hope her, mother is all right."

They walked in the condo, and there was Ms. Cotton. She looked extremely surprised to see La'Roc. "Hi, Ms. Cotton, you look so surprised. Is something wrong?"

"No, I am glad to see you. I tried to call your cell, but the calls kept going straight to voice mail. I spoke to Ms. Holiday, and she said that you were in court. That is why I looked so surprised. I wasn't expecting to see you so soon."

"I'm glad you are back, Ms. Cotton. How is your mom?"

"My mother passed away two weeks ago. That is the reason I am back so soon. I want to thank you for the money you gave me before I left that day. My mother was so very sick I cried so much I have no more tears left. All of my tears are buried with my mother."

At that moment, she looked like a little lost child. La'Roc took her in her arms and held her as they cried together.

Ms. Cotton turned to wipe her eyes. "Ms. Rose, I'm sorry. I didn't mean to cry. I guess I left some tears for you." They both smiled.

"Ms. Cotton, pack your clothes. You are going to Brooklyn with us. You need a vacation. Shawn has two extra bedrooms, one for you and one for Ms. Holiday. It will be like you and Ms. Holiday having a sleepover. Shawn has made his house into a home for all of us, including Paris and Biscuit."

Shawn was excited about the idea of them all being together. La'Roc felt that Ms. Cotton needed this family's support after what she had gone through.

As they headed for Shawn's, La'Roc began to think about her own mother. She opened her pocketbook to get her cell to call her.

"Hello, Mom, how are you today?" she said when her mother answered.

"I'm doing just fine, baby. How are you?"

"I am good. I was just thinking about you and decided to give you a call. Mom, let's have lunch together tomorrow."

"Okay, baby, that sounds great. I will call your sister and see if she would like to come along."

"No. Mom, I'm making tomorrow your day."

Her mother began to laugh. "Thank you, baby, I will see you tomorrow. I'm going to play bingo tonight with my friend Emma. So wish me luck."

"Good luck, Mom. Oh, by the way, bring your friend Emma to lunch with you tomorrow."

"Okay, I will ask her to come."

She ended the call and put her cell back into her purse.

Shawn said "Baby, when we get home, I will make you a nice drink to calm you down. You've had a long day dealing with the court, Kelly, and my sister."

"Okay, sweetheart, that sounds like a plan. Shawn, you're so considerate of other people's feeling. Take Ms. Cotton's situation, you felt her pain. I saw the pain throughout your facial expression. Baby, you always take excellent care of me and my little ones. I love you for that."

As soon as they arrived in Brooklyn, she was really happy to see Shawn's brownstone. They parked. Paris and Biscuit were in the window, wagging their tails and whining because they were excited to see La'Roc. Ms. Cotton was ecstatic to see Paris. "Oh my, what is this? Paris, you have a playmate?" Biscuit jumped on her.

La'Roc and Shawn decided to go upstairs before Alex arrived.

Shawn laid across his beautiful king-size round bed looking good as always.

"Hi, Sexiful, are you coming to join me, sweetie?" he asked.

"Yes, just for a few minutes. Hold me. That will make me feel better."

"Sweetheart, you only have to ask me once. Come into my arms and let daddy hold you."

In the big round bed, they became as one. They fell asleep in each other's arms.

They woke up around four thirty and decided to take a shower. About an hour later, Alex arrived. Shawn invited Alex in with a handshake and a bump of the shoulder. "Glad you could make it." Alex had his laptop and his black briefcase to review Shawn's case that was presented today in court.

"She's is in the backyard with her babies. Come, let's go out back."

"Hi, La'Roc, are you having fun?" Alex asked when he saw her playing in the grass with her puppies.

"Yes, Alex, I am in seventh heaven with my three babies. The third baby is Shawn." They all laughed. Ms. Cotton served drinks while Ms. Holiday served the appetizers. Alex and La'Roc went over the case while Shawn cooked fish, steak, and chicken on the grill. They were having a wonderful time. Alex called his girlfriend, Tyesha, and invited her to come over. Chantal, Denise, and their boyfriends stopped by to have dinner also.

They played cards, danced, and told jokes about each other.

Around midnight, everybody left the party, leaving Shawn and La'Roc alone. Ms. Cotton and Ms. Holiday decided to take Paris and Biscuit and headed upstairs to their bedrooms. Shawn and La'Roc headed for the shower. They talked for a while, and then fell asleep in each other's arms.

Shawn's doorbell started to buzz.

"Shawn, wake up, baby, someone is at the door."

Shawn got up, rubbing his eyes as he walked to the door. "Who is it?"

The voice on the other side of the door responded, "Shawn, somebody has really fucked up your gate."

"Baby, what's wrong?" La'Roc asked.

"Johnny from across the street said that someone destroyed my gate. Don't worry about it. I will handle it. I think I know who did this." La'Roc had a pretty good hunch herself. Shawn's phone started to ring off the hook.

"Shawn, baby, please don't answer the phone. It's Kelly. Let the voice mail pick it up. We need all the proof we can get." She asked Shawn to call the police and report the incident about his gate.

The police arrived and asked all kinds of questions about the broken gate. Shawn explained what had transpired earlier on during that day. La'Roc stayed in the background until they started to back Shawn into a corner.

"Do you have any drugs on you? Is that how you make your money to pay for this house?" she heard the police saying.

She stepped out from the hallway. "I am his lawyer. Before you accuse him of anything, please read him his rights. You're way off base. Now clean up your fucking act and get the hell out of this man's house. Who is your supervisor? You can tell me now, or you can tell the judge when I take your ass to court. Let me give you my name." She gave him a card with her information.

"Oh shit, man," one of the officers said, "that's you? You're the best lawyer in the state. Hey man, let me apologize." He stuck his hand out to Shawn. Shawn didn't extend his hand.

"Please leave my home. I should bring charges up on your ass. If my lawyer wasn't here, where would I be now?"

"Don't worry, baby, it won't happen again." La'Roc looked at the officer. "That is correct, Officer Miller. When you go back to the precinct, please tell them if Mr. Parker calls again to report any type of incident, please respond with respect. If not, I will have your badge. If you think I won't take your badge, just try me."

Once they left, Shawn was very upset because of the way the police treated him in front of his woman.

They were up the rest of that night, talking about the gate that had been destroyed. They couldn't say for sure who had done it, but they both had their suspicions. Shawn continued to apologize about the incident.

Something just didn't seem right. La'Roc had a gut feeling that Shawn wasn't telling her the truth about his detachment from his son's mother, that something was wrong with that picture. As a lawyer, she felt she had insights on when clients were holding something back and being dishonest. If Shawn had been lying to her, he would be very sorry because she would not be made a fool of.

She warned him on several occasions on the subject of honesty.

La'Roc was hoping that her gut feeling was wrong this time. *I love Shawn, but if he lies to me, it's over. I will continue to be his lawyer as long as he needs me. I will be there for him as his lawyer as well as his friend*, she thought to herself.

She kissed him good night and went to sleep.

He said, "Good night, Sexiful. I love you so much. I need to make things right with you so you will have no doubts about our love. Because, Sexiful, you are the only one for me. I'm sorry about tonight." Shawn pulled her close to him so she could rest her head on his chest while they both slept.

As she was sleeping, she dreamt about her first day as a lawyer. She was terrified of not knowing what to expect in a courtroom.

As she stood behind the solid lectern, facing the judge, her head felt like it was on fire.

Fifteen minutes earlier, a jury had found her client guilty of armed robbery. After brief arguments, the judge had pronounced a sentence on James Robertson, a tall eighteen-year-old black male. The reason

James was sentenced because he wasn't being honest with her as his lawyer. That day, she made a promise to herself that she would never lose another case on the assumption that a client hadn't lied to her.

When they awoke the next morning, Shawn and La'Roc got dressed and went for a walk in downtown Brooklyn. That was her first time walking around downtown Brooklyn. She enjoyed herself. They stopped and had breakfast and some chocolate ice cream, which was one of her favorites. Afterward, they took the long walk back to Shawn's brownstone hand in hand.

"Hey, babe, I'm going to the office for about three or four hours. I will call you as soon as I get there. Love you," Shawn said.

"Sweetheart, I'll be all right. Don't worry. You be careful and come back home safe. Love you."

He got in his car and drove off.

La'Roc decided to do some Pilates before going on her lunch date with her mother and Emma. After about an hour of exercise, she called her mother.

"Are you ready for our date?" she asked.

"Yes, I am. Emma is here already. We are just waiting on you."

La'Roc took a quick shower, then got in her BMW and headed to her mom's.

La'Roc, Geneva, and Emma decided on a restaurant called Smart Seafood for lunch. They got a booth quickly and chowed down on "Crab Fest." They enjoyed Sutter Home Moscato and laughed and talked about almost everything under the sun. They were having so much fun. La'Roc glanced at her wristwatch. She hadn't realized that they had been sitting in the restaurant for close to three hours. She was having such a blast with her mother. Her mind drifted back to Ms. Cotton and how she would feel if anything would ever happen to her mother. She decided at that moment that she would try and spend as much time with her mother and at least talk to her every day to let her know that she loved her.

After their lunch date, La'Roc dropped Geneva and Emma home, then headed to Manhattan. She wondered what happened to Shawn. It had been three hours since she last spoke to him on the phone. She decided to call his office. His office phone rang, but there was no answer; the machine picked up. She felt herself getting worried because of what happened the previous night. She wished like hell that she could prove that Kelly damaged Shawn's gate, but she had no proof that she did it.

On the way home, she decided to try Shawn again. No answer. La'Roc quickly pressed Redial. On the second ring, he finally picked up. "Hi, babe, I was just getting ready to call you."

"I called like four times, Shawn. I was worried about you. What happened?"

"I'm sorry, babe, I got caught up in something," he said. "Sexiful, what is your favorite color?"

"I really don't have a favorite color. You pick a color for me that you like," she answered.

"You look good in all colors. Come on, babe, give me a color."

"Okay, I like mint green and white together. That's a nice soft color."

"Okay, you got it."

La'Roc was curious. "Shawn, what are you doing?"

"Sexiful, I'm just trying to show my love after last night. I will see you in a bit."

"Okay, Shawn, I will see you later." They hung up; then she walked into her office to look over some cases. Shawn's surprise was still on her mind. She began reviewing the Sanchez case. His day in court was coming up, and she wanted to be ready.

After about an hour of going over documents, she thought she should take a break. She looked out of the window that was facing the landscape in the backyard. The backyard was so beautiful with the flowers, nice trees, and the nice barbecue pit that was surrounded by tables and chairs. She was thinking about the wonderful things he had accomplished in such a short time.

Hours passed with no word from Shawn. She decided to call his cell to see what was up. He didn't respond. She called his office; the answering machine picked up.

"Okay, that's it," she said aloud as she put on a pair of sweats and a tight tank and ran to her SUV. This was not like Shawn. Shawn was always on time.

She pulled off. She was driving like a bat out of hell; she arrived at Shawn's office in no time. As she pulled into the parking lot, Shawn and the police were walking out the door of Shawn's office. The police had Shawn in handcuffs.

She jumped out of her SUV, leaving it running and headed over to Shawn. "Officer, what's the problem? Mr. Parker is my client. What did he do, and you better have a good reason for having him in handcuffs." She looked at the officer's badge. "Officer Mott, please, you tell me what happened."

"Well, we got a call stating that Mr. Parker was involved in an incident last night and physically attacked a female in his parking lot at his office building."

"Would her name happen to be Kelly Brown? Mr. Parker was with me last night, and if you need proof, go and read the report that was taken by your fellow officers last night. There were an incident last night, but that occurred at Mr. Parker's home, around three this morning. Someone destroyed his property, and the police were called to his home. Check the report. Shawn couldn't have assaulted anyone. We just came in from California yesterday."

The officers decided to check out La'Roc's story and called over the dispatch to see if she was telling the truth. Moments later, her account was proven to be correct.

"Officer, is my client free to go?"

"Yes, he is free as a bird."

"Good," La'Roc said. "He will accept his apology now." She pointed to both police officers.

"We're sorry, Shawn."

"No, officers, that will not work. Try to apologize again—the correct way."

The officers did apologize to Shawn, "We apologize, Mr. Parker."

"I want this Kelly woman arrested for filing a false report too," La'Roc demanded. The police officers said they would look into it, got in their cruiser, and drove away. When they were gone, Shawn walked over to La'Roc's car and turned off the engine.

"Shawn, why didn't you call me?" she asked.

"I really didn't think it would go this far. Baby, I'm sorry. Forgive me, please?"

"Don't worry about it, baby. I just want you to be safe. Shawn, you know what you have to do? Cut all ties from Ms. Brown until we get this mess straightened out. She is trying to bring you down. We will make some arrangements about your support check for your son. Alex will handle that. He will make sure that your check gets to the appropriate place and also keep records of it."

"Baby, that would be great, and that way, I won't have to see Kelly."

"Shawn, this is what you want, right? Because once we get started in court, there's no turning back. Are you with me?"

"Baby, you are what I want, and I want Kelly to stay out of my life. I have a surprise at home waiting for you."

"What is it?" she asked. With all the commotion, she totally forgot he had mentioned something about a surprise.

"It's a surprise. I can't tell you. I'm surprised that Ms. Cotton or Ms. Holiday didn't tell you. They both know."

"Ms. Holiday and Ms. Cotton know about my surprise, and they didn't tell me?"

Shawn smiled and said, "Of course they do. I couldn't do it alone. Let's go."

On the way to Shawn's brownstone, they decided to stop and get some takeout. They ordered baked chicken, steamed fish, steamed vegetables, and a chocolate cake.

"I can't wait to get home and eat. This food smells delicious," La'Roc said. Shortly after, they pulled up in front of Shawn's place. He turned off the car, then reached over, went into the glove compartment, and took out a blindfold. He handed it to her. "Here, put this on."

As she put on the blindfold, he asked her if she loved him.

"I will answer your question when I see my surprise."

Once the blindfold was on, La'Roc could hear Shawn getting out the car. A few minutes later, he opened her door and helped her get out.

"You ready to see your surprise?" he whispered in her ear.

"Yes, I am," she answered. He pulled the blindfold from her face. When La'Roc opened her eyes and there before her was a mint green Hummer SUV.

++++++

She couldn't speak. She couldn't believe Shawn bought her a Hummer.

"Oh, Shawn, I love you so much. Thank you soooo much." She kissed him.

"Well, go check it out." He tossed her the keys. She ran to her new car and opened the door. Inside was immaculate. The interior was all white, and it looked spectacular. She hopped in the driver's side.

"Baby, you have to stop buying me things."

"Sexiful, please let me spoil you. I like buying you nice things. I like seeing your face light up like a little kid on Christmas Day."

He got in the passenger seat and watched her as she touched everything in the SUV. She smiled and leaned over and kissed him again. She loved this man already, but he was constantly finding ways to make her love him even more. She climbed over to the passenger seat and sat on top of him. He kissed her slow and passionately. They made love right there in her new SUV. Shawn made love to her like there was no tomorrow. He knew every spot to touch to make her want more of him.

After they finished their lovemaking, they went inside and took a shower. Shawn suggested they have their food on the floor in the den set up like a picnic. La'Roc agreed. They spread a sheet on the floor and laid out their food. They took some of the fluffy pillows off Shawn's couch and used those as their seats. After their mini picnic, they retired to bed.

Shawn woke up first the next morning. He opted to let La'Roc get some sleep, and she didn't mind a bit. Hours later, she finally decided it was time to get out of bed. After heading to the bathroom to wash her face and brush her teeth, she found Shawn downstairs on the kitchen phone.

"Afternoon, babe," he said to her and planted a kiss on her forehead. She smiled and returned the greeting. "I'm going to put some food on the grill real quick for lunch. What do you want?" he asked.

"Anything you make is fine with me, babe," La'Roc answered.

"Okay, just relax in the den. I'll come get you when everything is ready."

Shortly after she went into the den, Shawn came in. "I'll be right back, okay?"

"Shawn, wait a minute, where are you going?" La'Roc asked.

"I have to make a run. I need something for the food."

"Well, fine, just hurry up," she said jokingly. He kissed her cheek and headed out the door.

Shawn was gone for almost an hour. Right as La'Roc picked up the phone to check on him, she heard him putting his keys in the door. She went to the door to greet him and see if he needed help with any of the bags, if he had any. To her surprise, when she opened the door, she saw Chantal, Denise, her sister, and her mother. Shawn walked up the steps behind them.

"Oh my goodness, what are you all doing here?" La'Roc asked.

Chantal went on to explain how Shawn had planned the whole thing as a way to surprise her. La'Roc let them in and went upstairs to get dressed. She put on a pair of tight-fitting Levi's jeans and a white tank top. She threw on her flip-flops and headed back downstairs. She was in a relaxed mood today.

"So what's up with you, girl?" Chantal and Denise asked when their friend joined them again. La'Roc told them all about her last two days and the drama that filled them. She then told them about Shawn's surprise. Her friends screamed with delight.

"You got to show us this!" Denise exclaimed.

La'Roc led her friends outside to show off her new ride courtesy of her man.

While her friends were checking out her new SUV, La'Roc's phone began to ring.

"Hello, who is this?" she said without looking at her caller ID.

"Hi, Mom, this is your daughter."

"Hey, Courtney," she said, an instant smile spread across her face. "Oh, baby, I wish you were here to celebrate with me and Shawn."

"What are you celebrating?"

"Shawn just bought me a new Hummer. It's mint green with white interior. It is beautiful. I have to drive it to California to show it off. You're going to love it, I promise you."

La'Roc talked with her daughter for a few more minutes before they hung up.

"Love you, and tell my grandson to call me tonight."

"Okay, will do. Love you, Mom," Courtney said, and then hung up.

La'Roc and her friends made their way to the backyard. Shawn was throwing down on the grill. He had fish, chicken, steaks, a variety of seafood, champagne, beer, and cakes. And he had other goodies to server. He had everything; the group danced, played games, and ate a lot of food.

About four hours into the cookout, Shawn stopped the music and called for everyone's attention. He asked La'Roc to join him in front of her friends and family.

"La'Roc Rose. I just want you to know that I love you. The love I have for you run so deep, words cannot explain it. But I will try, I will try and make you understand how much I care, love, and respect you. There's only one way I can think that may give you just a piece of how deeply in love with you I am." Shawn then got on his knees, pulled out a diamond ring, and proposed to La'Roc. She began shaking and crying. She was speechless; much to everyone's surprise; she turned and ran into the house. Shawn ran after her. When he caught her, he pulled her into his strong arms. He kissed her and asked again. "Baby I love, will you marry me? We don't have to get married tomorrow. I just want us to be engaged."

"I love you too, Shawn, you know that. But you should have talked to me before you announced it. I was humiliated because we had not discussed this engagement thing."

"Baby, I am really, really sorry."

Tears began to stream down La'Roc's face. She looked Shawn in the eyes as she said, "Shawn, I love you, and I would be glad to be engaged to you. Nothing would please me more than to be Mrs. Parker."

Shawn smiled and picked her up as he kissed her a thousand times. "I'm sorry if I embarrassed you. That wasn't my intention. My intention was to show my love to you in front of your close friends and family. I want your family to approve of me."

"Shawn, you don't have to prove anything to my family. The only things they want from you are respect and just love and take care of me."

He picked her up and carried her back out to the backyard. "She said yes!" he screamed with pure joy. Everyone clapped, whistled, and screamed.

Chantal decided to make a toast. "May you guys have a happy life together? Live always in love. And, Shawn, if you hurt her in any kind of way, you will have to answer to me," she joked. "This woman is my best friend, and I love her dearly. Love you guys."

Denise quickly chimed in on the toast. "Good luck to my best friend and her future husband. Shawn, I love that woman standing next to you. Please treat her nice. Shawn, if she comes to me with a story that you have hurt her, I will hunt you down like an animal, and when I find you, it will not be a pretty sight. Love you much."

The cookout continued; the ladies gathered around La'Roc to check out her new diamond ring. The festivities lasted well on into the night. It was after three in the morning before Shawn and La'Roc actually touched their bed. Making love that night was out of the question. They were too tired. They just fell across the bed, and she slept with her head on his chest.

The next morning, when La'Roc woke up, the first thing she did was call her daughter to share with her the good news. Courtney was ecstatic for her mother. "Mom, I wasn't going to tell you, but I'll actually be in New York this afternoon. My job is sending me on a medical conference. I'm sitting in the airport now waiting to board my flight." La'Roc was overjoyed. She couldn't wait to see her daughter.

After her phone call, she went to the bathroom and did her normal morning routine of washing her face and brushing her teeth. Afterward, she headed to her exercise room that Shawn had made just for her. She worked out for an hour and a half.

Shawn snuck up behind her and smacked her on the butt. She was startled. She turned around and hit him playfully.

"Morning," he said.

She stopped exercising and told him about Courtney's plans.

"That's great."

They talked for hours about Courtney and about the cookout the previous evening. She loved the fact that they could just sit in the house and be completely content with each other. A few hours later, La'Roc's phone began to ring. It was Alex; he wanted to update her on his progress with the Sanchez case.

"Well, we did it again. Mr. Sanchez is a freeman. The court decided to throw out the case. I found out that the prosecutor was bribing jurors. He offered to pay them a pretty penny to come back with a guilty verdict. One honest juror out of the bunch contacted me and told me the whole story. Once the judge heard that, out went the case."

"Wow," La'Roc said. "That guy really has a thing for Mr. Sanchez, huh."

"It would appear so. He has a meeting with the bar tomorrow afternoon. I'm pretty sure he's going to be disbarred. I can't say I feel sorry for the officers," Alex said nonchalantly. They discussed the case for a little while longer. Alex was leaving the courtroom on his cell; La'Roc decided to tell him about Shawn's proposal. He congratulated her and asked for her to pass the message on to Shawn before he ended their phone call.

Shawn made them a tuna sandwich for lunch. She made a few phone calls, one of which was to her condo in Manhattan to check up on her housekeepers as well as Paris and Biscuit. After she was assured that everything was fine, La'Roc decided to take a short nap.

"Babe, wake up. Courtney is on the phone." Shawn was waking her up. She felt as if she was only asleep for a few minutes, but when she looked at the clock on Shawn's Cablevision box, she realized she had been asleep close to two hours. She took the phone from Shawn and spoke to her daughter. Courtney wanted to inform her that she had landed and wanted to meet her at Shawn's place. La'Roc gave her Shawn's address information, and they hung up.

"Is everything okay?" Shawn asked.

"Yeah, she's on her way over here to visit with us." La'Roc got up and got dressed. She had a few items of clothing still at Shawn's place since they returned from California. Shortly after, Shawn's doorbell rang.

"That must be Courtney," La'Roc said to herself. She walked to the front door and opened it. There stood Courtney, Justin, Jordan, and Devon. She couldn't believe it. "Oh my goodness, why didn't you tell me my grandson was coming too?" she looked at Courtney.

"Come on, Mom. I couldn't ruin the entire surprise," Courtney said.

La'Roc grabbed her grandson and hugged him tightly. She then did the same to Courtney and Jordan. "Hi, Justin, It's nice seeing you again."

"Same to you, Ms. Rose," Justin said politely. Shawn walked up to the door and greeted everyone. He grabbed Courtney's bag and helped her get inside. Justin and Devon followed.

They all sat in the den and caught up with everything that had taken place since they last saw each other in California. La'Roc told them all about her victory with the Sanchez case. That brought them up to the conversation of dirty people in law enforcement. Shawn brought up the incident with the cops the night someone destroyed his fence. They talked for about thirty minutes before Courtney announced that she was hungry.

"Come on, you guys, let's go out to eat. Shawn took me to this wonderful place a few days ago. Their baked chicken is to die for."

"Okay, Mom. I want to drive your Hummer," Courtney said.

La'Roc chuckled. "Well dang, can I drive it first? Maybe, just maybe, I will let you drive on the way back from getting the food."

Courtney agreed as she smiled from ear to ear.

The ladies decided to drive together in the Hummer, while the guys rode in a separate car. When they were all ready to go, Shawn led the way in the Lexus SUV. As they drove on, La'Roc couldn't believe how smoothly the Hummer drove. "Oh my god, Courtney, I cannot wait until you drive this machine. It drives so beautifully. Maybe I will drive you guys back to California," she joked. As they pulled into the restaurant, La'Roc noticed Shawn, Devon, Justin, and Jordan standing outside. Shawn was smiling from ear to ear.

Shawn walked over to her. "You look so cute getting out of that big truck. How you like driving your new Hummer, baby?"

"Shawn, the hummer drives better than my Lexus. It is an improvement from driving the BMW." She kissed Shawn on his cheek. They all walked into the restaurant; Shawn and La'Roc were hand in hand.

They spent about an hour in the restaurant, eating and drinking. When it was time to go, they headed to their cars. La'Roc tossed Courtney the Hummer keys. An instant grin came across her face. As they headed for the expressway, Courtney drove with the music playing, sunroof open, and her hair blowing in the wind just like her mother.

As they drove, La'Roc's cell phone rang. It was Shawn.

"What's up?" she asked.

"They need me to come into the office for a few. Pull over so the guys can ride with you. I'll catch up as soon as I'm done."

La'Roc instructed her daughter to pull over on the shoulder, and the swap was fast. They decided to head to Manhattan to La'Roc's condo.

When they arrived, Paris and Biscuit were excited to see their mommy as she was them. Courtney decided to take them for a walk. La'Roc instantly thought back to when Courtney was in high school. She had two puppies, Champ and Sheba. They both shared a certain love for dogs. Like mother, like daughter.

Ms. Cotton and Ms. Holiday spent a few minutes checking out La'Roc's new ride. The guys relaxed inside and watched television. She thought to call Shawn to let him know that they were in Manhattan, so when he was ready to leave, he didn't go to Brooklyn to an empty brownstone. After she hung up the phone, she went upstarts to get into her Jacuzzi. She had missed getting into it since she had been at Shawn's place. Ms. Cotton came in to check on her.

"I'm fine, Ms. Cotton. How are you? We haven't had much time to talk since you've been back. So much has been going on."

Ms. Cotton went and poured La'Roc a drink and sat on the edge of the Jacuzzi. The two women spent some time catching up. La'Roc could tell that something was off with her housekeeper. She just wasn't the same since the passing of her mother.

"Ms. Cotton, are you all right? Ms. Cotton, please let me in so I can help you. There is no need to be ashamed of your emotions. You must let it out. I am here for you. As a matter of fact, we are all here for you. Ms. Cotton, you are a part of this family. I know that you are hurting, and I want to help you get though this tough period." Instantly, Ms. Cotton began bawling.

"Ms. Rose, I miss her so much. How can I stop the pain?"

La'Roc felt a wave of grief flood over her. No matter how old you got and how grown you thought you were, you would always need your parents. She couldn't imagine the pain that Ms. Cotton was feeling. She couldn't picture her life without her mother. So she had absolutely no answer to Ms. Cotton's question.

"I'm going to make an appointment for you to see my therapist. Would you like that?"

"Ms. Rose, I cannot let you do that for me. You've done enough."

"Ms. Cotton, how long have I known you?"

"Ten years," she answered.

"I will not listen to another word. You will start counseling tomorrow. Trust me, it will help. You cannot keep those emotions bottled up inside."

Ms. Cotton smiled, and La'Roc took that as a way of her saying that she had accepted her help. Ms. Cotton excused herself and left. La'Roc got out of the Jacuzzi before she turned into a prune. As she was getting dressed, there was a knock on her door. "Come in."

It was Ms. Holiday. "Ms. Rose, may I speak to you about Ms. Cotton?"

"Yes, Ms. Holiday, what is it? Did something happen that I should know about?"

Ms. Holiday walked in and quietly closed the door behind her. "She is suffering something awful. Sometimes I hear her crying in the bathroom, and she cries herself to sleep at night. I asked her if there was something I could do to help her. She never responds to me. She just continues to cry. Please help her, Ms. Rose. She will listen to you because she loves you."

"Don't worry, Ms. Holiday. I'm making an appointment for her to see Dr. Paula Green. Thank you, Ms. Holiday, for helping Ms. Cotton get through this horrible pain that she has endured. She is so alone without her family not being here to support her. We are all that she has." Ms. Holiday nodded her head.

There was another knock on the door, and Courtney entered. Ms. Holiday exited the room so they could have some privacy.

"Mom, what's going on? Are you okay?"

"Yes, baby, I'm fine. I'm just a little worried about Ms. Cotton."

"What's wrong?"

"She just lost her mother, and she is taking it very hard. I am scheduling an appointment for her to speak with my therapist. I just hope that will work. I really don't like seeing her so down and out."

"She will be all right," Courtney assured her mother.

La'Roc called Dr. Green and scheduled an appointment for Ms. Cotton. Dr. Paula Green had been La'Roc's therapist for years, and she was a dear friend of Chantal. The appointment was set up for the next day at 10:30 a.m.

Courtney left her mother to continue getting dressed. Shawn called to say that he was on his way to the condo. He was just leaving the office. When he arrived, the group ordered takeout and watched movies in the den. Shortly after, everyone was beat and decided to retire to their rooms. La'Roc and Shawn talked about her concerns about Ms. Cotton; she told him about the appointment she had set up for her and how she hoped that it helped. They took a quick shower together and went to bed.

La'Roc's night was full of nightmares about losing her mother. She had Ms. Cotton on her mind heavily. She thought about how much she loved her mother. She had no clue what she would do without her. She was her glue that always held her together when she felt she was going to fall apart.

Although it was late and she knew her mother wouldn't answer, she decided to call and leave a message on her mother's answering machine. In her message, she relayed how much she loved her and cherished her. After that was done, she fell asleep.

The next morning she reached over to kiss Shawn, and to her surprise, he wasn't there. She walked out the room, and the sweet scent of breakfast invaded her nose.

"Good morning, baby, I'm making you breakfast. Please go back to bed. I want to give you breakfast in bed."

She smiled. "Okay, but hurry, remember I have that appointment at 10:30 a.m. with Ms. Cotton."

After Shawn served her a delicious breakfast in bed, she and Ms. Cotton got ready to be on their way for Ms. Cotton's therapist appointment.

"Hey, Mom, before you leave, can I get the keys to the Lexus. I want to take Devon to visit Grandma."

La'Roc smiled. "I'm sure she would love that. Shawn has the keys. He'll give them to you."

Courtney walked away to retrieve the keys from Shawn.

La'Roc and Ms. Cotton got in the Hummer, and off they went. They arrived at the doctor's office on time. Ms. Cotton was hesitant. She didn't really care for therapists. She explained to La'Roc that a friend of hers was on prescription medication that a therapist gave to her, and she died from complications. La'Roc reassured her that nothing was going to happen to her. This was to help her, and if necessary, she would do all the research she could do in the event that Dr. Green decided to give her medication. After a few more minutes of coaxing, Ms. Cotton went inside. Shortly after, Ms. Cotton walked into Dr. Green's office.

"Ms. Cotton wished for me to share the results of this meeting with you. It would appear that she trusts you very much. Ms. Cotton has great admiration for you. She needs all the support that you can give her. I would like for her to visit me in my office three times per week. Ms. Rose, she is very depressed. She needs a strong foundation at this hard time."

La'Roc rubbed Ms. Cotton's shoulders. "We will take care of her. Whatever she needs, I will get it for her. Ms. Cotton is very important to me. She is family, she is my family."

At the end of their meeting, the doctor handed Ms. Cotton a prescription for Zoloft to help with her depression. Ms. Cotton was reluctant, but in the end, she took the paper.

Dr. Green said, "La'Roc, how have you been? It has been awhile since we had a session."

"I am good, Paula. We need to talk about what has happened to me since the last time we had a session. It is all good. I am very happy."

"La'Roc, you look happy. Let's have lunch soon."

When they arrived back at La'Roc's place, Ms. Cotton expressed her gratitude and gave La'Roc a tight hug.

"Ms. Cotton, you are a part of this family. I really mean that."

"Thank you," she said. "If you don't mind, Ms. Rose, I would like to take a quick nap."

La'Roc agreed, and Ms. Cotton went to her room. Her house was empty. Her daughter and grandson were at her mother's house. Ms. Holiday and the puppies were out. She had no idea where Shawn and Jordan could be; she chalked it up to them having men's day out, and that was perfectly fine with her. At the moment, she just wanted to be alone, just her and her thoughts. She stripped and lounged in her bed; she stared at her ceiling until she drifted off to sleep. She woke up to Shawn crawling in the bed beside her.

"Hey, sleepyhead," he said once he realized that she woke up. "How did the appointment go with Ms. Cotton?"

"It was good. The doctor wants to see her three times a week, and she gave her something for her depression. I actually think Ms. Cotton enjoyed talking to her. She's in her room, taking a nap now. Where were you all day?"

"I was a little bit of everywhere. Jordan wanted to check up on some old friends of his. One thing led to another, and before we knew it, time flew by." He put his arms around her. "Are Courtney and Devon still with your mom?"

La'Roc nodded. "They should be back soon."

They talked a while longer until they heard Courtney and Devon come in. They went downstairs to greet them and to see how their visit with Geneva went. Jordan decided to prepare dinner for the group. The ladies set up one of the tables. Jordan cooked up a wonderful meal of fried chicken, potato salad, baked macaroni and cheese, and steamed vegetables. They all sat around the family table. Even Ms. Holiday and Ms. Cotton joined in.

"So when are you guys going back to California?" Shawn asked as he stuffed a forkful of mac and cheese in his mouth.

"We leave in two days. Tomorrow, I probably won't see you guys. I'll be at my medical conference all day. I was hoping that we would be able to have a get-together before we left town though," Courtney answered.

"That's a great idea, sweetie. What did you have in mind?" La'Roc asked. "I was thinking something like a pool party. Maybe we could have it at your place in Westchester. Devon and I haven't been there in a while."

"Yeah, Grandma, that sounds cool," Devon added.

"Well then, it's settled. Pool party it is," La'Roc agreed. They talked while they ate. Ms. Cotton seemed to be enjoying herself. It looked like she was coming around to being her old self again. After dinner, Jordan offered to clean up and give Ms. Holiday and Ms. Cotton the night off. After making sure that he was certain he wanted to do that, they went into Paris and Biscuit's room to play with them for a while before turning in for the night. Everyone else retired to their rooms. Courtney told them she would be seeing them most likely around dinnertime. The conference was scheduled to last all day. Shawn was tired from running around with Jordan all afternoon. He fell asleep first. La'Roc decided to have a glass of wine and watch a movie. She was asleep before the movie ended.

Waking up to Shawn singing in the shower wasn't ideal, but La'Roc thought it was funny. She got up and joined her man in the shower. "Oh, it's you in here? I thought it was one of the dogs in here howling." She began to laugh.

"Oh, you got jokes?" He splashed water in her face. They had a mini water fight in the shower. He grabbed her and pulled her close; he kissed her softly and told her he loved her.

"I know," La'Roc said. That was one thing she was certain of. She knew Shawn was in love with her.

They all decided to head to the supermarket to get whatever was necessary for the pool party that afternoon. They drove to Costco and picked up so much stuff. "Make sure you get that red velvet cake," Shawn said. La'Roc picked up two cakes. After the outing, they all headed over to Westchester to clean up the place to get it ready for the pool party. They also made whatever phone calls were necessary to invite a few people. La'Roc, Ms. Holiday, Ms. Cotton, and the puppies were in the Hummer; and the guys were in the Lexus. Courtney had borrowed the BMW to attend her conference and said that she would meet them at the town house.

Ms. Holiday and Ms. Cotton had the place spotless in no time, and before long, people were showing up. Chantal, Denise, Mike, and John were among the first people to arrive. Shawn and Jordan were holding down the grill as usual, and Devon was in charge of the music.

"So when is the wedding date?" Denise asked.

La'Roc shrugged her shoulders. "We haven't even talked about that yet. That's not happening for at least another two years, so you have a while to wait. Shawn has to deal with all his issues and make sure they are cleared up before anyone walks down that aisle."

"Come on, girl. What are you waiting for? You got a good man on your hands."

"Denise, don't rush her. She knows what she's doing," Chantal said in defending La'Roc.

"Not for nothing, but I want to make sure that Shawn is sure. I mean, it all sounds good and nice now. But remember, I am older than him. Who's to say in a few years, he won't change his mind. When I get married, I'm not planning on getting divorced. No way. My parents didn't get divorced and neither will I."

Denise rolled her eyes to the sky. "La'Roc, please, okay? He knew how old you were when he asked you to marry him. Why would that change all of a sudden?" The friends went back and forth with each other. It was Chantal and La'Roc against Denise. Denise knew she wouldn't win this argument.

Courtney pulled up with Justin. He had been visiting with his half brother. She wanted to help decorate the pool site. There were lights surrounding the pool. In the end, everything looked beautiful. La'Roc's sister and mother arrived shortly after the decorations were put up.

"Is there anything that I can do?" her sister asked.

"Yeah, you can relax and enjoy yourself."

Her sister sat next to her niece, and they chatted.

La'Roc noticed that Justin wasn't his usual happy-go-lucky self. He was on his cell phone most of the time, and when he finally did hang up, he looked as if he was in a daze. She asked her daughter if Justin was all right.

"Yes, Mom, I think so. He hasn't said anything to me about being upset about anything. He will be okay."

The party was great; everyone had a blast, and around two o'clock in the morning, everything was wrapped up. Shawn and La'Roc headed upstairs, took their showers, and went to sleep.

La'Roc woke up early the next day. She knew that it wouldn't be long before Courtney, Devon, and Jordan were on that plane heading back to California. She wanted them to stay, but she knew she was being selfish because they had their own lives to live. She spent the rest of the time with them, talking in the den until it was time to take them to the airport. The drive to LaGuardia was a somber one. When they got there, Shawn helped them unload their luggage, and he said his good-byes. La'Roc took a little while longer. She hugged her daughter and grandson for longer than they would have liked. She just really didn't want them to go. She loved having them around. She gave Justin a hug and told him to take good care of her daughter. He said he would. Jordan walked up to her and gave her a hug.

"I will call you as soon as we land. Love you, Sexiful. Oh, am I supposed to call you Sexiful?" he laughed.

"Yeah, man, I'll allow you to call her Sexiful this time. Please don't make it a habit." They both laughed and hugged each other. Then it was time for them to board the plane.

As La'Roc and Shawn drove home, she began to cry nonstop. Shawn tried to calm her down, but she was too far gone with the tears. It hadn't been ten minutes, and she missed her daughter and grandson terribly. It was at that moment that she decided she would go into semiretirement. She would let Alex handle the brunt of the cases and go to court. She would do all the research and behind-the-scenes stuff. That way, she would have more time to travel to see her family.

La'Roc and her family returned to her town house. Paris and Biscuit jumped all over her. During the last few days, she hadn't really paid them much attention with all the visitors she had. Shawn said that he was needed at the office and took off.

She saw Ms. Cotton and asked her how her visit went with Dr. Green.

"It was a wonderful visit. Thank you so much for recommending her. You were right. I just needed to talk about it. I'm beginning to feel much better."

"Ms. Cotton, I'm happy that it is working for you. Are you taking your medication?"

"Yes, Ms. Rose, and thank you again. I thank you and Ms. Holiday for helping me."

La'Roc decided to call Alex and tell him about her plans for semiretirement. He thought it was a good idea, and he supported her decision. After talking with her lawyer, she poured herself a glass of champagne, grabbed a book, and decided to take a relaxing soak. She heard a knock at the door; she told the person on the other side of the door that it was unlocked.

"Sorry to bother you, Ms. Rose, but Shawn was on the phone. He just wanted me to tell you that he is running a bit late and would be home about thirty minutes later than usual."

"That's fine, Ms. Holiday, thanks for the message." Ms. Holiday nodded, and then left the room.

After she finished soaking, she moisturized her body, put on a pair of her silk pajamas, and laid in her bed. She decided to watch a movie, but before it ended, she had fallen asleep.

It was three in the morning when she heard Shawn coming in.

"Shawn, what took you so long to get home? Think about it before you answer me."

"Nothing, babe, me and some of the guys went for drinks after work." La'Roc didn't respond; she just turned over and went back to sleep.

The next morning, she got out of bed, took a shower, got dressed, and went downstairs. When she got to the kitchen, Ms. Holiday and Ms. Cotton were preparing breakfast; she was still a bit upset with Shawn's selfish act the night before. He could have at least had the courtesy to call her and let her know that he would be more than thirty minutes late as he had originally told her. After she had her breakfast, she decided to go to her office and arrange some things for Alex to pick up. She left a note on the desk for Shawn and went on her way. Before she got to her destination, Shawn was calling her on her cell.

"Shawn, I really don't want to talk to you right now. I just need some space. You can understand that, right?"

"Sexiful, we need to talk about last night. I am sorry about that, but I need to talk to you."

"Okay, Shawn, we'll talk about it some other time, but not today. Please respect my wishes."

"Please give me just a few minutes to explain what happened last night. I was really with some of the guys from work. I was not out with other women because I love only you. You must believe me."

"Shawn, I am on the expressway. I will talk to you soon."

"Sexiful, wait." She hung up before he could get another word in. He called back, but she didn't answer.

Music blasting and with her speeding, she didn't hear the siren blowing. She glanced in her rearview mirror and spotted the police car in full speed. The police were speeding like her car was on fire. She pulled over, sat in the Hummer, and waited until the police reached her car.

"Hi, Officer, is something wrong?"

"I don't know yet. Maybe you can enlighten me as to why you were speeding. That would be a great help if you can explain to me why you were ignoring the speed limit."

"I am sorry, Officer, was I speeding?" she asked.

"May I see your driver's license and registration?" Officer Rodriquez reached for her credentials.

"Your name is La'Roc Rose. Were you the lawyer that recently handled an officer's case? His name was Sanchez."

La'Roc smiled and confidently said, "Yes, I am."

"Ms. Rose, it is a pleasure meeting you. My wife is in law school. You're all she talks about. Her dream is to work with you one day."

"She's in luck. I'm looking for some good lawyers to work in my firm. Here take my card. Tell her to give me a buzz when she graduates." La'Roc handed him one of her business cards.

"Thank you so much, and thank you for the wonderful job you did on our fellow brother-in-blue case. Drive carefully." The officer went back to his cruiser and sped away.

She continued on her way to her office where she spent most of the afternoon getting things ready for Alex. When she was just about to finish up, Shawn called her.

"Where are you, babe?"

"I'm at my office getting ready to leave now and head to Westchester."

"I'll meet you there," he said and hung up. He cut her off before she could object. When she pulled up, he was already there, waiting for her outside. She parked the car and walked to her front door. Shawn hugged her around her waist.

"Shawn, please get off me."

"Sexiful, please talk to me, baby. Whatever I've done, I'm sorry."

"Shawn, it's not about what you did. It's what you didn't do, and if you can't figure that out, then we don't need to be together. I'm not angry with you because you were out with the boys. I want you to go out with your friends. I want you to enjoy your life, so when we do get married, if we get married, you won't have to say, 'What if.'" She looked Shawn in his eyes and said, "I just need a day to myself. Okay? I need some space."

"Okay," Shawn said. "I'll call you."

La'Roc huffed. La'Roc said "yeah, Shawn, just like you called me last night?" she shot back.

It was at that moment that Shawn realized the mistake he had made. "I get it. I'm sorry. I should have called and told you. But it's been so long since I was with the boys that I lost track of time. Baby, I don't want to lose you over some bullshit like that. I'm sorry."

"I heard you, Shawn, now hear me. I need some space."

Shawn said he would respect her wishes. He turned and walked away. He climbed into his SUV and pulled off.

La'Roc entered her house and went straight to the Jacuzzi. She poured herself a glass of wine and soaked while she sipped and listened to the slow music that oozed from her speakers.

She soaked, but her mind was on Shawn. She figured that she had overreacted and decided to call him to apologize. Dialing Shawn's number, she smiled to herself because this was the first time she had to apologize to anyone. It was something new to her.

"Hello, beautiful, is everything all right?"

"Shawn, I just want to say I am so sorry about my behavior. Baby, I don't know what happened to me and why I came off like that. Acting like a child was very immature on my part. Forgive me, Mr. Parker."

"Sexiful, of course I forgive you. I love you." She smiled to herself. "I want to come over and hold you in my arms and tell you face-to-face how sorry I am about last night."

"That would be great. I will be waiting for you upstairs in our favorite place," she said.

"Okay, babe, I'm on my way ASAP."

Her phone began to ring again. She thought it was Shawn calling back. When she checked the caller ID, it was Courtney.

"Hey, babe, what's up?"

"Mom, Justin is in the hospital. He's in critical condition. He was shot five times during a robbery in his father's store." Courtney was hysterical on the other end.

La'Roc "Oh my god, baby. Is he all right? I'm going to call Jordan."

"Mom, I called him already. He is on his way." Courtney couldn't stop crying.

"Baby, I need you to calm down. Justin needs you to be strong for him now. You hear me?" La'Roc said, trying to calm Courtney down. "Be by his side and wait for Jordan to get there. I'm going to see if I can get a flight out there tonight."

"Okay, Mom," Courtney said to her mother through tears. "I'll call you right back."

They hung up, and La'Roc immediately began making phone calls to the airport.

Shawn walked in as she was purchasing her ticket.

"Hi, beautiful, miss me?" She ran into his arms with tears in her eyes. "What's wrong, Sexiful? Talk to me."

"My daughter just called me, crying hysterically. Justin was shot several times during a holdup at his father's store. He's in critical condition, and Courtney seems like she's on the verge of losing it herself. I'm going there tonight to be with my daughter."

"Sexiful, you know if you need me, I'm right there with you."

"Good because I don't think I can handle seeing my daughter all broken up if something is to happen to Justin." La'Roc purchased two tickets to California.

She began throwing things in her suitcases. Shawn packed whatever clothes he had at La'Roc's place. She briefly explained the situation to Ms. Holiday and Ms. Cotton. She called her car service to transport them to the airport. When they arrived, La'Roc and Shawn were on their way. On their way, La'Roc called and spoke to Courtney again. She told her that she was on her way to the airport and would be getting there tonight. Courtney sounded a bit better, but La'Roc could still hear the worry in her voice. Justin was still unresponsive, and they wouldn't let her see him. While they talked, Jordan arrived. She let Courtney go so that Jordan could comfort her.

When they got to the airport, Shawn got the tickets and checked in the bags. Once they boarded the plane, Shawn held her close to his chest. The sound of his beating heart put her to sleep.

He woke her up when it was time to get off the plane. La'Roc was happy that she managed to sleep the whole flight. She didn't know how she would deal with sitting on the plane anxious to speak to her daughter and couldn't.

La'Roc called her daughter, but there was no answer. She left a message. "Courtney, this is your mother. Please answer your phone! We are on our way to the hospital. I need to know what floor Justin is on. Courtney, baby, please answer your cell and please call your mother."

Shawn grabbed their bags from the overhead bin. They walked to the airport exit, and La'Roc scanned the crowd with her eyes until she spotted a driver holding a sign with her name on it. She called Courtney again—still no response. Tears began to well in her eyes. Shawn hugged her and told her everything would be all right.

"I know. I'm just worried about my child. I want her to call me, Shawn. I need to hear from her. Let me know that she is all right."

"Baby, please, stop crying. She will be okay. Believe me, baby, she is going to be great. She is like her mother, smart and strong. Please don't worry, sweetheart. Babe, try Justin's cell. Maybe she has his phone."

As the driver loaded their suitcases, La'Roc tried Justin's number. Courtney answered. "Hi, mom."

"Courtney, baby, we're here. Which hospital are you guys at?"

When her daughter told her the info, La'Roc forwarded the info to the driver, and he pulled off.

When they arrived at the hospital, Courtney met them in the lobby. She stepped off the elevator looking every bit like a model. She was walking toward La'Roc with her long legs and a smile on her face. Her facial expression showed concern about Justin. "Hi, Mom, Hi, Shawn, I am so glad you guys are here." They hugged and cried. Devon followed behind his mother.

Devon ran to her and gave her a hug and gave Shawn a high five.

Devon looked at his mother and walked over to her. He pulled her into his long arms. "Mom, I am so sorry about what happened to Justin. Mom, please don't worry, he will be all right."

They all held hands for a few minutes and got in the elevator and went to the fourth floor to visit Justin.

Walking into Justin's room was a sight. He had tube in almost every hole in his body. La'Roc thought to herself, *If I can't stand to see him like that, I could just feel the hurt that my daughter must have been going through.* This was the man that she loved. For a moment, La'Roc saw Shawn stretched out on that table. She instantly felt nauseous. She grabbed his hand as tight as she could. Looking at Justin, everyone knew he was in bad shape.

Shortly after, a doctor walked in. "Mom, Shawn, this is Justin's doctor, Dr. Mitchells," Courtney introduced him. He took their hands and shook them firmly.

The doctor explained that one of the bullets had severed his spine; they were able to piece it back together, but the chances that he would walk again where nil. Another bullet went through his groin area. They did all they could, but the doctor concluded that he would never be able to have children. At that moment, Courtney wept as though La'Roc had never seen her cry before. La'Roc's heart was crushed. It killed her to see her daughter in so much pain.

Justin's father was out in the hall; he couldn't take seeing his son like that. La'Roc understood where he was coming from; she didn't know what she would do if something like that happened to her daughter or grandson. She pulled Courtney close and let her cry on her shoulder. She rubbed her back and stroked her hair. At that time, that was all she could do to comfort her. She and La'Roc knew that wasn't doing the job.

She could feel her phone vibrating in her pocket; she knew that it was Chantal and Denise. She left them both messages, just giving them the basics about the situation. She asked Shawn to take the phone and explain to them what had happened. She couldn't leave her daughter just then. Shawn called out to Devon who was waiting in the hallway. "Let's take a walk, little man, to get something cold to drink."

Courtney started crying uncontrollably. The more La'Roc tried to comfort her, the more she cried. She began trembling, and then suddenly, she fainted. The doctor ran back in the room and paged for nurses. La'Roc felt her world spinning. She couldn't handle it if anything happened to her daughter. After a few minutes, Courtney came to. The doctor gave her a sedative to calm her down. By the time Shawn and Devon returned to the room, Courtney was out like a light. The expression on Devon's face when he walked into the room and saw his mother on a hospital bed was that of sheer terror. He wanted to know what happened to his mother. La'Roc told him what happened and reassured him that she would be fine. She explained to him that his mother would need him more than ever before. "I understand. Shawn told me everything, and I will be here for her no matter what."

Shawn heard what happened, and he held her as tight as she could stand it.

She loved his strong arms around her. She felt so protected when she was in arms.

After hours of waiting around for any signs of improvement from Justin, there was nothing. The doctors told them that he was heavily sedated, and he most likely wouldn't wake up until the next day.

"Shawn, let's take her back to the hotel with us tonight. I don't feel that she should be alone. She needs her family tonight." He agreed.

They left the room so that Courtney would have some privacy. A few moments later, she walked out. Her eyes were bloodshot, and dried tears stained her face. La'Roc pulled her in close to her. They all said good night to Justin and went on their way. The ride to the hotel was a quiet one. The only sound was the constant sniffle of Courtney's nose.

When they arrived at the hotel, La'Roc ran her daughter a warm bubble bath and encouraged her to just sit down for a soak. She sat on the toilet seat cover and stayed with her. From the bathroom, she heard Shawn's phone ring.

"Hello, who is this?" There was a pause. "What the hell you want from me?"

La'Roc excused herself from the bathroom and went to check on Shawn.

"That was Kelly on the phone," he said as soon as he saw her.

"What's the problem now?" La'Roc asked.

"She said she had to rush my son to the hospital. He has a high fever."

La'Roc looked at Shawn. "Do you believe her?" As she waited for his response, she remembers that he had changed his cell phone number. "How did she get the new number, Shawn?"

"I'm not sure. Must have been from the time I called her to check on my son."

For some reason, a wave of anger came over La'Roc. "I thought you said you hadn't been contacting her, Shawn."

"Sexiful, I only called her to check up on my son. Since all of this court stuff started happening, I haven't really talked to him. I missed him, so I called her to see if he was all right."

La'Roc was shocked. "Oh, so now I'm the reason you don't talk to your son? If you miss him so much, Shawn, then go back to New York and be with him. Leave now! I have my own child to take care of. I'm not stopping you from doing anything you want to do."

"Babe, I didn't mean it like that I assure you."

La'Roc cut him off. "Go, Shawn! Now! Devon will drive you back to the airport. Go be with your son."

Shawn tried to explain himself, but it was all in vain. La'Roc returned to the bathroom to be with her daughter. She decided not to tell her what just happened since she already had enough on her plate for one night.

Shawn sat on the bed and tried to find flights leaving out that night, but nothing was available until later on the next day. He explained that to La'Roc; she brushed him off. She tucked her daughter into bed and fell asleep at her side. The next morning, when she woke up, Shawn and Devon were gone. There was a note from Shawn, saying that he loved her, and they would talk when he got back. Courtney saw the note and asked her mother what had happened that caused him to return to New York so fast.

"Nothing, baby, his son got sick, so he just went to check on him is all. You ready to go see Justin?" she asked, quickly trying to change the subject off Shawn. Courtney said yes, and after they both had showered and dressed, they were on their way. Courtney called her son and told him to meet them at the hospital after he dropped off Shawn On the drive there, La'Roc's phone began to ring. She thought it was Shawn, but when she checked the caller ID, it was Denise. She told La'Roc that she and Chantal had just landed. They needed to make sure that both their best friend and their goddaughter were okay. They didn't like the way she sounded on their voice mail.

"We're on our way to the hospital now to see Justin. You can meet us there if you'd like." She gave them the address and room number to where Justin was, then continued on her way.

When they got to Justin's room, Dr. Mitchells was there. Courtney ran over to Justin. To her surprise, he was awake. He couldn't talk, but just to see his eyes open brought a wide smile across her face. La'Roc also saw that his eyes were open.

"Thank goodness," she whispered to herself.

Dr. Mitchells asked La'Roc to step outside with him. "Hello, Ms. Rose," he said once they were out of Courtney's earshot. "I thought it would be best to tell you first."

La'Roc felt sick to her stomach. She figured that whatever she was about to hear wouldn't be good.

"Justin is in pretty bad shape."

"What do you mean, Dr. Mitchells? His eyes are open now. That's better than he was doing yesterday."

He cut her off. "His eyes are open, yes, that's true, but don't let that mislead you. After several tests this morning, we aren't noticing any brain activity. We are afraid that he may have irreversible severe brain damage."

La'Roc's heart hit the floor. *Justin is going to be brain-dead? No, that couldn't be*, she thought to herself. She felt for her daughter and how she would feel once she heard this news. At that time, Chantal and Denise came off the elevator; they ran over to La'Roc and hugged and kissed her. They had a million and one questions. Dr. Mitchells excused himself and went on to complete his rounds.

"So what's going on?" Chantal asked.

La'Roc didn't know how to get the words out. "The doctor just told me that there is a possibility that Justin is going to be brain-dead. They know for sure that he won't walk again. My poor daughter, I don't want to be the one to tell her." She began to weep.

Her best friends grabbed her and hugged her tight. "Come on now, you can't break down. You have to be strong for Courtney," Denise said.

"And if you don't want to tell her the news, I will. She's my goddaughter, and I'm here for her no matter what." Chantal wiped La'Roc face, and the three of them entered the room. Courtney was talking to Justin. He had a blank stare on his face.

"Hey, what did Dr. Mitchells want, Mom?" La'Roc was lost for words.

"Hey, Courtney," Denise chimed in, "how's he doing today?" She changed the subject. She and Chantal walked over and hugged her. Courtney began to tell them what happened the night before.

La'Roc stayed off to the side. Her phone began to vibrate in the pocketbook. It was Shawn. She stepped out of the room and answered, "Hello, Shawn, I cannot talk to you right now. We are at the hospital. I will call you later." She hung up before he could say another word.

She was not ready to give Shawn her attention. She was still angry with him for giving Kelly his phone number and lying about talking to her. When she walked back into Justin's room, her daughter was kneeling on the side of his bed, crying. Chantal was trying to pull Courtney from the floor.

"Mommy, please help Justin. Please, Mommy!"

"What happened?" La'Roc asked Denise.

She went on to explain that while Courtney was speaking to him, he closed his eyes, and then she began to freak out. La'Roc picked Courtney up off the floor.

"Baby, Mommy is here for you. The doctors will do all they can to help Justin. Courtney, you have to take care of yourself. You have to eat so you can be strong to help Justin. Justin would want you to eat. You are killing yourself, baby. Please eat something. Come on; let's let him get some rest."

Chantal and Denise walked out of the room in tears.

It seemed like everything was falling apart at the time La'Roc needed her friends most. She and Shawn were crumbling slowly but surely, and her daughter was on the brink of losing her sanity. She looked at her daughter with tears in her eyes. *Oh, God, please give me the strength to help my child. She needs me so badly*, she silently prayed. "Come on, baby, let's get some air and let Justin rest."

Courtney agreed.

They went to Courtney's house. Denise made her some chicken soup. "Come on, Courtney, eat up," Denise said.

Courtney refused to eat and laid her head in her mother's lap as they lay on the couch.

There wasn't much that she could do for her daughter, and she knew that. She decided that her daughter needed to talk to someone professional. She needed a doctor who could talk to Courtney straight up without worrying about protecting her. A therapist would be able to talk to her straight and help her at the same time. She shared her thoughts with her daughter, and Courtney agreed.

"Chantal knows someone out here. Her name is Dr. Kim, and according to Chantal, she's great. I'll ask her to call her right away." La'Roc called for her friends and told them her idea. Chantal went to her phone right away and got the doctor on the phone. She told them that she got the doctor to come over right away. About an hour later, Dr. Kim arrived. "I am pleased to meet you, Ms. Rose," she said after Chantal had introduced them.

"It's a pleasure meeting you, Doctor. Right now, my daughter needs you. Please help my child get through this, and I will forever be grateful to you."

"I will try my best to help your daughter to the best of my ability. First, I need a bit of background information."

They sat in the kitchen with the doctor, and Denise stayed in the living room to comfort Courtney. La'Roc went on to explain what took place at Justin's father's store and what Dr. Mitchells had told her that morning.

After she had filled her in as much as she could, La'Roc led Dr. Kim to the living room and introduced her to Courtney. Dr. Kim asked for privacy. La'Roc, Chantal, and Denise went back to the kitchen.

"Don't worry. Courtney is in good hands now," Chantal said.

Denise poured them all a glass of wine, then asked for Shawn. "I thought you said he was here with you," she continued.

"He was here, but he flew back to New York to be with his son. His mother claimed he was in the hospital, and since Shawn blames me for being the reason he hadn't been seeing him, I asked him to leave."

"What?" her friends asked at the same time. She explained the incident that happened last night. While she was talking, Devon called and said he was on his way from dropping Shawn off. La'Roc told her grandson to meet them at Courtney's house. They hung up, and the women continued talking.

"La'Roc, after hearing what you said, I really don't think Shawn was trying to say that you're the reason he hadn't been seeing his son," Chantal said.

"Yeah, I agree. I think that this whole thing with Justin and Courtney had you a bit stressed out on Shawn. You can't blame him for wanting to talk to his son. He had no choice but to call her. He's a good father, and he missed his son. And I'm just being honest," Denise said.

Hearing her friends' point of views put things in perspective for La'Roc. How could she really have thought that Shawn wouldn't want to talk to his son? She concluded that she had overreacted and took her stress out on him.

Moments later, Devon walked in the house. He saw his grandmother and her two friends there and instantly asked for his mother. La'Roc explained to him that his mother was in the living room talking to someone that they all thought could help her.

"Is she going to be all right?" he asked.

"Yes, she'll be fine, honey. We all just have to be here to support her and be strong for her."

La'Roc's phone began to ring. "Hello, who is this?"

"Hi, baby, this is Shawn. I'm at the airport. I would like to see Courtney if you don't mind, and we need to talk. We have to talk."

La'Roc began to smile. "Okay, Shawn. We're at Courtney's place."

"See you soon, Sexiful." They hung up the phone.

"I'm assuming that was Shawn. You have that big-ass smile on your face," Denise said.

"Yeah, that was him. He's back in California, on his way over here now. I need him to know what's going on with me has nothing to do with him. He needs to know that I still love him."

"He knows that you love him, and he loves you. Shawn will be happy to help in any way that he can because he loves you both," Chantal said.

The women sipped their wine and talked for a while until Courtney and Dr. Kim joined them. Courtney had a smile on her face. She walked over to her mother and hugged her. She thanked Chantal for referring such a wonderful doctor. She explained that Dr. Kim told her that she had to hold it together for Justin. If she broke down, he wouldn't get better. It was okay to cry, but try not to do it in front of him. Her crying was his worry. He might interpret that as a sign that he wouldn't get better. She had to have faith and trust in the doctors, that they were doing all they could to help him. But if she was breaking down too, the time they spent taking care of her was time taken away from Justin.

Dr. Kim said she would go and visit Justin at the hospital and talk to his doctors. She would call if there were any updates. She wanted Courtney to stay home tonight and focus on getting herself better. She said her good-byes and then exited.

"Mom, are you okay?" Devon asked.

"Yes, Devon. I'm sorry if I scared you, babe."

"Mom, that's okay. I'm good as long as you are."

Shawn rang the doorbell at that moment. Devon went and opened the door. Shawn walked in, and a slight smile spread across La'Roc's face. He walked over, and before he could say anything, La'Roc blurted out her apology. "I'm sorry, babe, for treating you the way I have for the last few days. It was wrong of me to think that you wouldn't have any contact with your son. I know that you weren't blaming me, but with everything that was going on here, I was just stressed, and I took it out on you. I'm sorry."

He kissed her softly. "It's all good. How's Courtney?"

La'Roc told him that she had just spoken with a therapist and she was feeling a little better than yesterday. He asked about Justin, and she told him what Dr. Mitchells had shared with her earlier. Her phone began to ring. She checked the caller ID. It was Jordan. She hadn't seen him since she arrived last night. With all the commotion, she hadn't even realized it.

"Hey, Jordan, what's up?" She paused. (He asked about Courtney) "She's fine. What's wrong? You don't sound like yourself. Talk to me."

She paused again. "Oh, Jordan, I am so sorry. I'm on my way." She looked at Shawn. "Jordan . . . fine, okay. Please make sure you call me."

When she hung up, Shawn asked her what had happened. "Jordan said his mother passed away. She had a stroke."

"Damn," Shawn said.

La'Roc began to cry. "When is this all going to end? I can't take the people I love being hurt."

Shawn reached out his arms, and she fell right into them without hesitation.

She decided not to share the news with Courtney yet. She would wait a few days. Jordan's mom was like a grandmother to her. La'Roc just didn't think she would be able to deal with her death at this time.

They joined everyone in the living room, and they all talked and had a good time. They tried to keep Courtney's mind off Justin. After about two hours, they were all tired and decided to go to sleep. Courtney wanted to visit Justin early the next morning.

La'Roc and Shawn slept in the living room on Courtney's pull-out couch.

The next morning, La'Roc's phone woke her up. It was Dr. Mitchells from the hospital. An instant sensation of panic took over. She picked up the phone, preparing to hear bad news.

"Morning, Ms. Rose. I wasn't sure if you were going to make it in today, and I didn't know who else to call."

"What's going on, Dr. Mitchells?" she asked. She just wanted him to cut to the chase.

"I've known Justin and his family for quite some time now. I took care of his mother before she succumbed to her injuries after her terrible car accident. So I know that, besides his father, Justin has no one other than his father. I'm just a bit concerned that his father hasn't been around to visit. Ms. Rose, I've tried to contact him numerous times. This isn't like him. I explained to you what we think we've found yesterday, and I thought it would be best that Justin had someone around him. You and your daughter seem to care a great deal about him. That is why I chose to call you."

"Don't worry, Dr. Mitchells, we're on our way. Thank you for calling." She ended the call and went to her daughter's room. To her surprise, she wasn't there. She heard the shower running in the upstairs bathroom and assumed she was taking a shower. She did tell everyone from last night that she wanted to get an early start today. She went back to the living room where her suitcase was and decided to get dressed so she would be ready when her daughter got out of the shower. After Courtney got dressed, she and La'Roc were on their way. Everyone else said they would meet them there after they showered and dressed.

They all visited with Justin for about three hours. Dr. Mitchells explained to them that he had shown significant progress throughout the night. He was recovering, and his brain began displaying some action. He still wouldn't be able to walk again. That was still great news to everyone. They all smiled and hugged each other.

They decided to go out to eat. Courtney had gotten her appetite back. La'Roc told her daughter about Dr. Mitchells not being able to contact Justin's father. She asked her to please see if she could get in touch with him. Courtney did as her mother asked. She dialed his number, but there was no answer. She left him a message, updating him on Justin, and asked if he would please visit him. After they ate, they went back to Courtney's house.

A week had passed since Justin's incident. Courtney and her family went to visit him every day. As the days progressed, Justin made significant improvements. He was able to sit up with assistance and talk. He wasn't able to walk because he was paralyzed from the waist down, but the wheelchair helped him to get around. Courtney couldn't have been happier, and La'Roc was fine now that her daughter was better. Jordan had also been by to visit. He was feeling better. He had decided to grieve for his mother alone. He didn't want to burden anyone or add any more stress.

Things still hadn't been the same between La'Roc and Shawn. She wanted him, but she didn't want him. She knew she had to make a decision soon about where their future together stood. Right now, she thought it was best that everything be brought to a standstill. There was a nagging voice in the back of her head that wouldn't go away. Although she understood why Shawn had called Kelly, she could not understand why he couldn't tell her. Shawn had a restraining order on her, and he was breeching that agreement. He was contacting her behind her back. It wasn't so much the contact that bothered La'Roc; it was the sneaking around that he was doing. This little lie led her to think what else he had been keeping from her. Kelly couldn't have this baby fast enough. La'Roc wanted to know the results badly.

Her thoughts took her to all sorts of places. *What would I do if Shawn was the father of Kelly's unborn baby?* She thought to herself. She wasn't sure if she could be with a man who cheated and fathered a baby while he was with her, much less be married to him.

"Hey, Mom, is everything okay? You're pretty quiet." The sound of Courtney's voice brought her back to reality.

"Yes, I'm fine." They were in Justin's hospital room. The doctor was preparing him for discharge. La'Roc and Courtney had been talking during the course of the last week about plans for Justin once he was released from the hospital. He wouldn't be able to go home. He would need a helper. Courtney offered for him to stay with her, but La'Roc wouldn't hear of it. "That's too much work for one person to handle," she said. After going back and forth, Justin and Courtney agreed it would be best for everyone if the two of them went back to New York with her and stayed awhile. La'Roc made all the necessary arrangements with the rehabilitation center that Justin would be going to in New York.

A few days later, they were all on the plane heading to New York. When they landed, they took Justin to the center. Courtney decided to stay with Justin on his first night in rehab.

La'Roc's first stop after leaving them was a visit to her mother. When she reached her mother's town house, she was digging in her flower garden.

"Hi, Mother dear, miss me?" she asked, smiling. She was so happy to see her.

"Hey, baby, how is Justin doing?"

"He is doing just fine. What have you been doing with your time since I've gone?"

"I have been worrying about Courtney and Devon," her mother said honestly.

"You can stop worrying. They are here, and they will be staying for a long while."

"Good, that's great. How's Shawn?"

"He's fine, Mom. He's at work." La'Roc didn't feel the need to drag her mother into her and Shawn's idiotic chaos. Nor did she feel like explaining anything and getting lectured.

She talked with her mom a long while as they sat at the little table in her garden. Her mom called it her "private place." And boy was it good to have some peace and quiet. After the hectic couple of weeks that she had, this was just what she needed. The entire time she was talking with her mother, her phone was vibrating. She figured it was Shawn and decided to make him wait. She was talking to her mother and enjoying every minute of it. After another hour of talking to her mother, it was time to leave. She kissed her good-bye. As she walked to her car, she checked her phone. She was wrong about the caller. It wasn't Shawn; it was Chantal and Denise. She called Chantal first.

"Hey, what's up? Sorry, I didn't pick up the phone. I was visiting with my mom, spending some quality time with her."

"Hi, girlfriend, have you talked to Denise?"

"No. I was going to call her after I hang up with you. What's up?"

"Girl, Roger is in the hospital. He is in a terrible condition."

She was shocked. "Why? What happened?"

"Denise and I heard that he was attacked by some crack heads."

"Chantal, what the hell are you talking about? What do you mean? Crack heads?"

"Just what I said, he is a fucking crack head."

La'Roc couldn't believe what she was hearing. She decided she would go to the hospital and see what was going on for herself.

La'Roc jumped in her car and headed to the place where Chantal said Roger would be. When she got there, she asked a nurse what Roger Harrison's room number was. The nurse gave her directions to Mr. Harrison's room. When she entered the room, she had to ask the nurse if she was sure she showed her the right room. He was completely unrecognizable. She walked over to his bed and shook her head with concern. She was apprehensive about trying to wake him. She stared at her ex-boyfriend. Even though they didn't get along, she would never want to see him the way he was now, all broken and beaten. Chantal and Denise showed up at the hospital.

"Hi, girlfriend, wow, what the fuck happened to him?" asked Denise.

"Oh shit! Somebody fucked him up," shouted Chantal.

La'Roc turned to her friends. "Please have some respect. I'm glad you both are here, but I will not have you making jokes about him. You guys understand that, right?" She knew that they didn't like him, but the way they were acting was totally out of line. Chantal and Denise both apologized.

A doctor walked in. "Hello, I'm Dr. Daniel Shepherd. May I ask who you are?"

La'Roc shook his hand. "Hello, my name is La'Roc Rose. I am a friend of the family. We came as soon as we heard the news."

"Oh. Ms. Rose, Mr. Harrison gave your name as next of kin, but he went into his coma before we could get a phone number."

La'Roc was shocked to hear that she was Roger's next of kin. He explained to her that Roger had internal hemorrhaging in his head as well as his lower part of his body. He lost over 40 percent of his blood. She looked over to Roger and was full of pity. Roger started to move his fingers on his right hand. She ran to his bedside. She called his name, and he moved his finger again. She smiled. "Hey, it seems like Roger is waking up."

Dr. Daniels shook his head. "No, Ms. Rose that is an involuntary movement from the medication." She sighed. She asked the doctor how Roger ended up in the hospital. "Roger was brought in by the police. They found him lying on the sidewalk in front of a crack den on 116th Street. He was alone, and he was nude. The police don't have any more information than that."

"Thank you, Dr. Daniels, for all of your help."

"Ms. Rose, there is nothing that you can do here. If there are any changes, I will give you a call. Just give me your number."

She left her number with the doctor, and then turned her attention back to Roger. She walked over to him and gently kissed his forehead. Chantal, Denise, and La'Roc left the hospital very quietly. Her friends knew that La'Roc was hurting for Roger. Roger and La'Roc did have a past together, and her friends understood her pain. They all went to La'Roc's condo in Manhattan. Ten minutes after arriving, Shawn was calling her. She didn't feel like talking to Shawn at that time, so she didn't answer the call. She felt that she had to focus on helping Roger. Shawn will just have to wait with his bullshit. Her phone continued to ring until she gave up and answered the phone.

"Yes, Shawn, what is it? Right now I am busy, so whatever you have to say, say it fast."

"Baby, I miss you, please talk to me."

"Not right now, I have a case I am working on. I will get back to you as soon as I can."

Chantal made drinks, and all three sat down to enjoy a stiff drink.

"How's Justin doing?" Denise asked, cutting through the tension that was heavy in the air.

"He's doing fine. Courtney is at the rehabilitation center with him now."

La'Roc's phone began to ring again. Chantal, who was close to the phone, checked the caller ID. "If that is Shawn, just ignore the call. I'm really not in the mood to talk to him."

"It's not Shawn. It's Roger's doctor."

La'Roc jumped to her feet and grabbed the phone. "I will take it in the den," she said, and then excused herself. "Hello, Doctor, how is Mr. Harrison?" she said once she answered. "I am sorry, Ms. Rose, Mr. Harrison passed away about thirty minutes ago. I am very sorry. We did all we could. Ms. Rose, you have my great sympathy. If there's anything I can do, please do not hesitate to ask."

Her jaw dropped; she was in utter disbelief. She hung up the phone and went back to where Chantal and Denise were. She told them that Roger had passed away. They both shook their heads in silence. Just like that, the heavy tension loomed over them again.

The next few days, La'Roc occupied herself with arranging Roger's funeral.

La'Roc contacted his family, over twenty-five showed up for the burial, and they were all looking for money. To her surprise, Roger had left her in charge of everything—his house, his money. Everything in his will he instructed her on how to split the money with his mother and sister. He left his brothers absolutely nothing.

The service was beautiful. He was buried in a bronze coffin. The church was decorated in tons of red, white, and black roses. It was a beautiful funeral, something Roger would have loved.

There was still no information on who had killed Roger. La'Roc was sure someone knew what happened. On the streets of New York, however, everyone lived by the secret law of "snitches get stitches." Everyone kept their mouth shut. No one wanted to be the next one to end up like Roger.

After the service, La'Roc headed to her place in Westchester. Driving home, La'Roc had some time to think about her and Shawn's complicated relationship. She popped in one of her favorite CDs, "What Will It Be" by Deeyah. She was driving north on Highway 95, she was speeding as usual, listening to her music, and thinking about Shawn. She definitely cared about what happened to him and what his future held. As she was speeding up Highway 95, traffic seemed to be coming to a standstill. She was wondering what was slowing her down. She switched on her GPS. The monitor on the GPS showed there was an accident farther up Highway 95. She cursed out loud, "Shit! What the hell."

It would take her two hours to get home.

She took out her cell to call Ms. Holiday. She informed her that she was on her way home, but the traffic was backed up like hell.

"Ms. Rose, Mr. Parker called. He said that he tried to call, but your phone went straight into voice mail. He asked me to tell you to call him please."

"Thank you, Ms. Holiday. If he calls again, tell him that I'll call him as soon as I reach home. How are my babies doing? Give Ms. Cotton my love. I missed you guys. See you soon, bye for now."

Looking at her cell, she noticed that she had a missed call and one message.

She checked the missed call and message; they were both from Shawn. Her phone rang again. It was Alex. "Hi, Alex, what's up?"

"Hello, partner, just wanted to touch basic with you. Sorry to hear about Roger. That was a tragedy. Roger had his ways, but he didn't have to go that way. He didn't deserve the way he expired."

"Alex, as soon as you have some free time, can you start digging into Roger's murder case. I will not let something like murder slide through the cracks."

"I'm on it, La'Roc. I will call you soon. Keep safe."

When La'Roc got home, she was greeted by Paris and Biscuit. Seeing them made her forget all about her issues. After she played with her babies for close to an hour, she went upstairs to the gym to have a nice long workout and to do some Pilates. Afterward, La'Roc relaxed in her whirlpool bath with her drink in hand.

She checked her phone, which she had left in her bedroom. She had a missed call from Shawn. She decided to call him back. When they spoke, he told her that he loved her and he needed to see her. He damn near begged. La'Roc decided to let him come up to Westchester. Her heart was telling her to give him another chance, but her mind was telling her to forget about Shawn. How could she forget about Shawn Parker?

La'Roc moisturized her body and then poured a glass of wine while she waited for Shawn. While she relaxed in her favorite chair, she decided to call Courtney.

"Hi, baby, how is it going?"

"Hey, Mom, I was about to call you. What are you doing, playing with your babies?"

"I have a date tonight with Shawn." She never told Courtney about her and Shawn's tribulations; she had enough on her mind with Justin recovering. They talked for a little while about Justin and how he was adjusting to the center. As her daughter described it, the center was a beautiful place with adequate staff that seemed very sincere in their efforts to help Justin. "That's great, Courtney. Let me talk to Devon."

She talked to her grandson for a short while. She finally decided it was time to bring up something that had been on her mind for a while now. "Devon, I understand the reason for you not going back to college this semester. However, it is time for you to get your act together. You need to get back in school."

"I have a surprise for you, Grandma. I'm going to law school. I've already sent in my applications."

"That's great news, baby. Once you graduate, Devon, you can take over my practice."

They all said their good nights; then La'Roc walked over to her walk-in closet to get dressed for her date. She dressed in a pair of white shorts and tank top to show off her toned arms. Shawn loved for her to show off her arms. La'Roc pulled her hair up in a ponytail, which made her look like a young girl.

As she put the finishing touches on her hair, Ms. Cotton announced that Shawn had arrived. La'Roc heard Shawn talking to Ms. Holiday and Ms. Cotton for a while.

"We're fine, Mr. Parker, it is nice to see you." Paris and Biscuit were also happy to see Shawn. He played with the two puppies while he waited for La'Roc to come downstairs.

When she walked down the stairs, the sight of Shawn playing with her babies brought an instant smile across her face. He looked up, and he was as gorgeous as ever. *How could I ever think of letting this handsome man go?* she asked herself. They greeted each other with a hug and a kiss.

His arms felt so strong; he seemed to be stronger than before.

La'Roc played with her babies for a few minutes, and they were taken to their bedroom by Ms. Holiday and Ms. Cotton. She and Shawn said good night to the babies.

Shawn made drinks for the two of them. As he handed over hers, he looked at her with love in his eyes, and she wanted to take him into her arms and love him to death. Before she could do that, she felt as if she had to make him understand that what he did was a disappointment to her and very selfish on his part. Shawn promised her that she was the only one for him. He apologized for violating the court order that he had against his son's mother and that he would never hurt her again. The sincerity in his voice, along with the look in his eyes, made La'Roc believe him. She and Shawn talked for hours.

"Sexiful, I missed you, please let's try our love again. Baby, whatever I did, it doesn't mean that I don't love you. Baby, I love you more than I love myself. I just need you to trust me, just this once."

"Shawn, I love you too." He held her in his arms as tight as he could, like she was literally afraid to let her go again. They kissed each other passionately.

That night, Shawn and La'Roc made love like there would be no other night for them to be together. La'Roc was overly excited to be with her soul mate once again.

Afterward, they took showers; Shawn lifted La'Roc into his arms and carried her to bed. They both slept in each other's arms all night.

The next morning, Shawn's phone alarm woke them up.

"Baby, where are you going? It's six thirty in the morning. Go back to sleep," La'Roc said.

"I will be back for lunch. I have an appointment to sell a house at ten. I want to get there before the client does to get everything set up. Sexiful, just remember that I love you."

"All right, sweetheart, I'll be here waiting for you, okay, sweets. I love you too."

Shawn kissed her on the forehead, and then left for work, and La'Roc fell off to sleep.

Not too long after Shawn left, her cell phone ring woke her up. It was Alex. "Alex, what's wrong?" La'Roc had a bad feeling; Alex never usually called that early.

"Partner, I have some bad news."

"What is it, Alex? Tell me, you know how I hate to wait."

"Well, partner, they just arrested Shawn at a house that he was showing to a buyer. Shawn called me and asked me to call you. I will fill you in when you arrive."

He told her they would meet at the Sixty-seventh Precinct. She jumped up and got dressed. La'Roc texted her two best friends: "Meet me at the Sixty-seventh Precinct. I will explain later."

She ran to her car and drove away like a speeding bullet.

La'Roc arrived at the precinct within the hour after the phone call Alex made to her. As she parked, she saw Chantal and Denise walking up. She was escorted to where they were holding Shawn. When she saw him, he was in handcuffs looking like a little boy that was stealing cookies from a cookie jar. He looked scared and confused.

La'Roc pulled Alex to the side and asked him to tell her what actually happened.

"Shawn was showing a man named Mr. Johnston a home when Ms. Brown approached the building and started calling Shawn's name. He walked over to the window and saw Ms. Brown and asked her to leave. She refused to leave. He left the window and walked up the stairs. She ran into the coop and ran up the stairs behind him. Mr. Johnston waited downstairs. He said he heard an argument but couldn't make out all the words. He says he heard Shawn ask Ms. Brown to leave several times. Next thing he knew, she was falling down the stairs. It's unclear on how she fell. He said, 'I cannot say that Mr. Parker was responsible for her falling. I did not see him push her. Mr. Johnston said he did not see what actually happened upstairs.' Shawn's statement will tell you everything, and I believe him."

They all sat around the small table getting Shawn's statement. La'Roc looked at her soul mate with sadness in her eyes. "As your lawyer, I will have to take your statement now."

"Sexiful, when can I leave this place?" Shawn asked, looking at her.

"First of all, we have to go in front of the judge. After we meet with the judge, he will hopefully set bail. Shawn, please do not be disappointed if he doesn't set bail. Shawn, you know the justice system is very tricky."

Alex's phone began to ring. He stepped in the corner and answered his phone. Two minutes later, he joined them at the table. "That was the hospital. Ms. Brown is in a coma." Shawn put his head down.

La'Roc knew that it would be his word against hers. There were no witnesses; the only person present at the time was the potential buyer, and he really wasn't much help.

"Shawn, you have to tell us exactly what happened. Start from the top." Shawn took a deep breath and started, "I was working at one of my sites in Manhattan. The address where I was working is 3467 Marble Hill Drive. I was setting everything up before my buyer arrived for his appointment.

"Mr. Johnston showed up about an hour after I did. We started walking around the coop. He seemed to like what he saw. He laughed and said, 'Give me the paperwork, I am ready to buy. This place is just what I needed for my family.' As I was handing him the papers to sign, I thought I heard someone call my name. Mr. Johnston stated that he also heard someone calling my name. Then he said he heard the sound of a door being opened. There were no locks on the doors being that the coop was not completed. That's when I saw Ms. Brown. I asked her to leave, she refused. I thought that if I just ignored her, she would get the hint and just leave. She didn't. Instead, she ran up behind me. When we were upstairs, I continued asking her to leave. After she threatened me a few times, she finally began to back away to leave. That's when she fell over the side of the railing. I tried to catch her, but I was too late. She fell backward over the rail. I ran back down the stairs where the buyer was standing over her. I thought that she was going to die right there. She fell two floors down. I called the 911. When they arrived, the paramedic began to work on her. Baby, it was horrible. The police arrived. They asked her what happened. She looked at me and, in a whispering weak voice, said, 'Shawn.' Mr. Johnston tried to tell the police what happened. One of the police officers said to him, 'He's going to need a damn good lawyer to get out of this. He better pray that she makes it.' I swear that is what happened." He looked at La'Roc, begging her with his eyes to believe him.

"Sweetheart, don't worry, we got this case. First thing, we got to get you out of here. Alex, if you don't mind, would you please go to the hospital to check on Ms. Brown?"

"Partner, I'm on it." He grabbed his briefcase and left. Chantal and Denise also decided to leave. Chantal thought she would serve a better purpose at the hospital since she was a doctor. The three of them left.

She opened her arms; he sat next to her and laid his head onto her lap and cried like a baby. "Baby, I am innocent, you have to know that. I cannot leave you. I cannot make it without you."

"Shawn, I believe you're innocent. I know that you did not push her, and remember, we do have a witness. I need to get some information from him. You do have his info, right?"

"Yes, everything is in my office. There is a set of keys in your kitchen, hanging by the outside door. Ms. Holiday knows where they are."

"Shawn, I have to leave you now. I need to make some phone calls. Shawn, the officer may have to put you in a holding cell for now. Just cooperate."

"Okay, baby."

La'Roc placed a phone call to Alex to get some information on Ms. Brown's condition.

"Partner, she is holding her own. She has tubes everywhere. She is in critical condition, and she is still in ICU. She had some internal bleeding and other complications. The report that I received was that they stopped the bleeding, but they could not save the fetus, and if she makes it, she will be paralyzed from her neck down." They spoke for a while longer; then she made a few more phone calls.

There was no way Shawn would be coming home tonight. He would have to wait until the next day before he was arraigned.

She went back inside to break the news to Shawn. She asked the officer if she could see Mr. Parker; she was granted permission to visit with Shawn as his lawyer.

She told him that he would have to spend the night in his holding cell and he would be arraigned in the morning. She also informed him of Ms. Brown's condition. She said good night and told him she would be back first thing in the morning.

When she got home, her head was pounding. She was feeling like she never felt before. She was scared, outraged, and frightened. She feared that Shawn could be facing jail time. She was praying to God that Kelly would pull through.

Alex was calling her phone. "Hey, partner, she is still in a coma. She has had three seizers in the last three hours. The family asked to call a priest. They seem to be giving up on Ms. Brown."

She informed Alex of Shawn's arraignment time; he promised he would be there. "Alex, before you come to court, please give a call to Mr. Johnston and set up an appointment to get his statement. We need that statement like yesterday. That statement from Mr. Johnston is Shawn's only chance of being free. Alex, if Ms. Brown dies and Mr. Johnston refuses to testify, we're in deep shit."

She had a hard time falling asleep that night. She forced herself to fall asleep so that tomorrow would hurry up and come.

The next morning, Alex woke her up extra early. He wanted her to take a ride with him to Mr. Johnston's house in case there were any questions that she would like to ask Mr. Johnston herself. She quickly showered and dressed. She grabbed one of Shawn's suits from her closet before she headed out the door.

They made the quick stop to Mr. Johnston's house and recorded his account of the event. Afterward, they headed to the hospital to talk with the doctors about Ms. Brown's condition. They then made their way to the courthouse. Shawn was in a holding cell waiting for them.

As they sat in at their place in the courtroom, the atmosphere was somber. No one spoke; they were all too deep in their own thoughts. La'Roc looked over to Alex, who looked a bit frightened. She leaned close to him and said, "Alex, everything is going to be all right. Don't look so sad. We will win this case, maybe not today, but we will win. Remember, I trained you very well. Alex, you're smart and well educated." She looked at her partner. "Alex, I made you a partner for a reason. The reason is you're a damn good lawyer. We're the best, so let's prove that to Shawn."

La'Roc had a dreadful feeling that Shawn was not going home today.

However, if that would happen, it would be unpleasant for Alex. Neither lawyer was usually nervous before a case, but being as it was Shawn on trial, that had them a bit worried. Shawn would be free eventually. She wasn't worried about him doing hard time; she just dreaded the idea of him spending any more nights in jail.

The arraignment lasted for close to two hours. The prosecutor dug up all types of dirt on Shawn. He presented the two times that the police were called on Shawn. La'Roc tried her hardest to explain the calls away. No one wanted to hear it. The problem was that it was Ms. Brown who had made the phone calls so the prosecution was playing it as though Shawn was an abuser. They indicted him on attempted murder and assault in the second degree. Shawn turned as white as a ghost. La'Roc's eyes instantly filled with tears. She couldn't dare look at him. It ended as La'Roc thought it would: Shawn would not be going home that day.

Shawn was transported to Upland Correctional Facility, fifty miles from New York.

La'Roc could not get the word *indicted* out of her mind.

She knew that she was going to get him freed; she would fight forever for that, but just the thought of her being away from him for the next several weeks was going to be hell.

"Alex, we have work to do."

"Okay, I'm ready to get my hands dirty."

They went over their plan for the trial. They saw that the prosecutor was going to play dirty. La'Roc made sure that Alex listened carefully as she spoke. She wanted him to get a copy of the restraining order that Shawn had against Ms. Brown so they could prove that she violated her restraning order. She also wanted him to get copies of the police reports that had been filed when she destroyed his gate. She wanted his voice mail messages with Ms. Brown threatening him transcribed. She also wanted the transcript from all their court proceedings that they had when they were going back and forth about their son. Last but not least, she wanted to make sure that Mr. Johnston would be testifying on Shawn's behalf. He was their key witness. As they outlined the case, they both began to feel a lot more confident about what they had.

La'Roc decided to go home to get into a hot bubble bath and have a drink.

She felt lonely in her house all alone. She called and checked on Ms. Cotton, Ms. Holiday, and her babies. "Ms. Cotton, I want you and Ms. Holiday to bring Paris and Biscuit down to the condo tomorrow. I will be in Manhattan working on Shawn's case. I will see you and my babies tomorrow."

"Okay, Ms. Rose, see you tomorrow."

La'Roc hung up the phone. She called her mother and spoke to her awhile. Her mother boosted her confidence even more. She told her that, for now, she needed to relax her mind. That way, she would be able to think clearly and think things all the way through. She called Courtney but didn't get an answer. She figured she was probably busy with Justin and left her a message. While having her drink, she called Jordan to check up on him. He answered in a sleepy voice, "Hello, hey, baby sister, what a pleasant surprise. Courtney told me what happened to Shawn. Who is his lawyer?"

"Why do you ask?"

"I asked because if he has you, he has nothing to worry about. He will walk a freeman," Jordan joked, trying to lighten the mood.

"Thanks for the confidence, brother. What's been going on with you? You so tired. Did I wake you?"

"Well, La'Roc, I was going to call you and tell you I have been sick. I did not call because I knew you were busy with Shawn's case. I can tell you now." He hesitated and then continued, "I've contacted HIV. I take about a hundred pills a day."

La'Roc's heart snapped; she started crying immediately. She couldn't stop her tears from falling or the room from spinning.

"I am sorry I didn't tell you, sis. La'Roc, just remember this, I will always love you, Chantal, and Denise. You guys are the three stooges."

La'Roc couldn't speak.

"This is why I really didn't want to tell you. You've had enough on your plate with Courtney and Justin, and now with Shawn. I just didn't want to add more stress. I don't want to be the straw that broke the camel's back."

"Jordan, how will I tell Courtney and Devon? This will crush them."

"I will be in New York next week to see all of you. I will tell them then. I want you to prepare my will and be my power of attorney. I also need to say my good-byes to all of my friends."

La'Roc stopped crying long enough to speak. "Don't talk like it's over, Jordan. You have to fight it." She began sobbing again.

"I'm trying," he said in a weak voice. "Listen, baby, I will see you next week. I'm tired. I need to rest."

She didn't want to hang up with him, but she knew that he was tired. "I love you, Jordan," she said.

"I love you too, La'Roc G. Rose, always and forever."

La'Roc cried for what seemed to be hours on end. She cried for everyone. She cried for everything that she'd gone through in the last few weeks. She cried for Ms. Cotton losing her mother. She cried for

Justin and the pain he must be feeling. She cried for Courtney; she cried for Devon. She cried for Roger. She cried for Jordan losing his mother, and now he was fighting for his own life. She cried and cried.

"Get yourself together, girl. You have got to be the glue. You have got to be strong and put this all back together. Come on. Get a hold of yourself," she said, talking to herself. She wiped away the tears and pressed on. She was La'Roc G. Rose. She was a strong, intelligent woman. As her confidence grew, she got out of the whirlpool and worked on Shawn's case. She found the best hospitals to treat HIV patients. She was going to win. She wouldn't lose Shawn's case, and she wouldn't lose Jordan to that disease without the strongest fight that anyone had ever put up.

Three months later, Kelly Brown was transferred to a rehabilitation center. Shawn was released on one-hundred-thousand-dollars bail from Upland Correctional Facility.

Courtney and Devon moved from California to La'Roc's condo in Manhattan, and Justin was out of the rehabilitation center living in a halfway house.

Courtney got a job in NYU as one of the head surgeons.

Devon was accepted to Coward University Law School. He began classes and working with Alex and La'Roc in her firm as an intern.

Everything was going smooth for now. But there was much more to do. La'Roc would not be stopped, and she would always press on. There are much more in store for La'Roc. First things first, she had to make sure that she won her baby's case. Shawn will be free.

Jordan would be working on Shawn's case to help free him. He would be the third lawyer on the case. La'Roc was very happy about that.

Shawn's court trial was the biggest challenge of La'Roc's career. This case was different from her other cases because this person she was defending was her soul mate and the best lover she ever had. Her rational for summary Alex power and Jordan Diaz, because she wanted the best Lawyers to work on Shawn's case. She requested Alex Power and her best friend Jordan Diaz.

Will Shawn be freed? Tell me after you read Sexiful 2.

You can read all about Shawn's case in Sexiful Rose part 2.

Coming soon, Sexiful part 2—it will be full of excitement.

Relationship ended, relationship beginning, marriage, and death. Will Shawn and La'Roc get married?

Read and find out if Shawn fathered Kelly Brown's son and unborn child. You will be surprised with the results.

Sexiful 2 is worth waiting for.

It will keep you on your toes and wanting more of Sexiful Rose and Shawn Parker.

www.ingramcontent.com/pod-product-compliance
Lightning Source LLC
LaVergne TN
LVHW091549060526
838200LV00036B/767